Praise for *Transorbital*

"Nathan Singer is what a writer is meant to be: daring, unique, original, and insightful. *Transorbital* proves it in spades."
—Reed Farrel Coleman,
New York Times bestselling author
of Robert B. Parker's *The Devil Wins*

"Nathan Singer's *Transorbital* pulses with a relentless momentum. Singer propels a strange, unsettling world reminiscent of William Burroughs's best work with the fierce urgency of a Michael Crichton science thriller. With *Transorbital,* Nathan Singer has once again proven himself the master of the literary pulp thriller."
—Steve Weddle, author of *Country Hardball*

"I love everything about this book. I love the cult of the Transorbitals and the circus freakiness of it all. Like an ice pick to the frontal lobe of conventional fiction, *Transorbital* is what happens when the brilliant mind of Nathan Singer is unleashed on one of medicine's most embarrassing periods."
—Bryon Quertermous, author of *Murder Boy*

TRANSORBITAL

BOOKS BY NATHAN SINGER

A Prayer for Dawn
Chasing the Wolf
In the Light of You
Transorbital
The Song in the Squall
Blackchurch Furnace

NATHAN SINGER

TRANSORBITAL

Copyright © 2015 by Nathan Singer
First Down & Out Books Edition August 2020

All rights reserved. No part of the book may be reproduced in any form or by any electronic or mechanical means, including information storage and retrieval systems, without permission in writing from the publisher, except by a reviewer who may quote brief passages in a review.

Down & Out Books
3959 Van Dyke Road, Suite 265
Lutz, FL 33558
DownAndOutBooks.com

The characters and events in this book are fictitious. Any similarity to real persons, living or dead, is coincidental and not intended by the author.

Cover design by Lance Wright

ISBN: 1-64396-112-8
ISBN-13: 978-1-64396-112-5

*For Julie, Wolf and Levi
for their endless patience and support*

Voici le temps des Assassins
—Arthur Rimbaud

PART ONE
PSYCHO SURGERY

CHAPTER 1

"Don't take one step closer! I'm gonna SPLIT THIS GODDAMN WHORE IN TWO!"

Dr. Freeman had been giving a lecture at the University of Louisville when word reached us that one of his patients was at home attempting to cleaver his own wife into bite-sized filets. Apparently the lady had recently become possessed by several demons, including, perhaps, Old Scratch himself. Dumb luck that.

You could say that we had arrived just in time, and good fortune was clearly on our side. We had no equipment on hand. But no worry. Doc and I had by that time developed quite a knack for improvisation. It really was almost like jazz.

"Officers!" Dr. Freeman announced through the police chief's bullhorn, "This is Doctor Walter Freeman! Mr. O'Dell is a patient of mine. Please do not harm him or do anything rash. I can handle this. Eugene? Eugene, can you hear me?"

"Doc?" a voice shouted from the upstairs bedroom of the decrepit farmhouse. "Doc, I gotta do it! Gertrude's got a devil inside her! I gotta cut it on outta her!"

"I understand," Dr. Freeman shouted. "Please just wait until I get in there."

"Uh…" the voice replied, "Well…OK, then."

There appeared to be no working electricity within the rustic, ramshackle dwelling. Chickens and piglets ran wild in the living room. The place smelled from the same.

"Unless I miss my guess," Dr. Freeman said to me, "There is likely no Frigidaire in the kitchen. Go in and check, please."

I did. The kitchen appeared to be from a century past at least. Black, cast-iron wood stove. Spinning wheel. Oak table covered in cracked, chipped bowls and pitchers. No Frigidaire.

"You're right, Doctor," I shouted back to him. "Just an ice box."

"Glorious day," he said. "You know what to do."

I reached inside the scuffed, wooden icebox, which contained little but a few cuts of unidentifiable meat wrapped in brown paper, and grabbed the ice pick out of the rapidly melting block.

"Please tell me," he asked as I returned to meet him at the bottom of the stairs, "is it a *Uline* pick?" His voice was positively giddy. I checked. It was indeed. "Could our luck be better?" he asked rhetorically, and with a broad smile.

"We don't have the electro-shock machine with us, though."

"True. Alas."

"No anesthetics."

"Hm."

"We won't be able to sterilize."

Dr. Freeman looked at me as if I had just kicked an angry skunk.

"My dear boy, did I just arrive here after you? I am plainly aware of the situation."

"Sorry, Doctor."

"Time is of the essence."

"It is, yes."

"And besides," he said, "I cannot be bothered with all of that *germ crap.*"

And so up the stairs we went. Once inside the bedroom we found poor, thin, apparently demon-infected Gertrude O'Dell safely blubbering into the shoulder of a young red-haired cop who looked as if he hadn't signed up for this sort of detail. Four other officers held their pistols dead set on Eugene, who stood aloft his own spring-damaged mattress, swinging his cleaver wildly in front of him.

"Doc!" Eugene hollered. "Make them cops give me Trudie! I gotta fix her! But quick!"

Four hammers clicked back in unison. Gertrude wailed and sobbed.

"Officers, please!" Dr. Freeman said. "Allow me! Eugene, Trudie is right here. She's not going anywhere. If anyone requires surgery, I shall take care of it. Understood?"

"But Doc!"

"Eugene, who is the doctor here, you or I? Please do come down from the bed and hand me the cleaver."

"I can't do that, Doc!"

"Eugene, do you really want to be shot by these good officers here?"

"Doc, you don't unnerstan'—"

"Hand me the cleaver. I will take care of the operation."

I looked over at Gertrude who had fallen into full-blown hysterics. The officer holding her looked frantically at me, then to Dr. Freeman, then back again. He reached for his holster, likely intent on shooting Dr. Freeman himself. I simply shook my head and he dutifully moved his hand back to Mrs. O'Dell's shoulder.

Finally, after much panting and casting about, Eugene dropped the cleaver. It clunked to the floor with the sharp blade cutting straight into the hard wood, handle upright. Freeman slowly helped Eugene down and laid his hands comfortingly upon the large man's arms.

"There we go. It's all going to be OK," Doc said. "All right? Listen to me, Eugene. I'm going to make everything better."

"But Doc, them demons—"

"I will make the demons go away. Is that clear, Eugene? Do you understand?"

Eugene nodded, nearly in tears.

"Y—…yes, Doc."

"Very well then. No need to worry. Everything will be just fine. Just fine indeed."

Dr. Freeman turned his head toward the cops and shouted, "Now!" They instantly lunged and grabbed a hold of Mr. O'Dell who at once began thrashing and spitting, cursing loudly.

"Freeman! Goddamn you! BURN IN HELL!"

Two cops grabbed Eugene's arms, two others grabbed his legs. They held him down flat against the bed. Dr. Freeman turned to me.

"The Uline, please," he said. I handed it to him and climbed onto the bed, kneeling, securing Eugene's head. He growled and attempted to bite the meaty part of my palms, but I held tight to his sweat-slick face.

"Please calm yourself, Eugene," Dr. Freeman said casually. "Let's not make this *unpleasant*." All four officers looked at me, each more nervous and ill at ease than the next, holding on to the thrashing, 265 lb. farmer as tightly as they were able. I smiled, attempting to reassure them that all was well.

"Doctor Freeman…" one of them said, but then had nothing more to add.

"Please don't let go, officers, no matter what," Freeman said, his eyes glittering with anticipation behind the perfect circles of his wire-rimmed spectacles. He removed his left shoe, held it in his right hand as a makeshift hammer, and leaned over astride Eugene who lay helpless, prone, and nearly immobile. With both thumbs I peeled back Eugene's eyelids, and Dr. Freeman pressed the pointed tip of the Uline ice pick directly above the right eye.

"*Mother Mary*," one of the cops gasped, his face draining to a deathly white. Dr. Freeman grinned wryly, visibly pleased by the reaction, and proceeded to hammer the metal point into the eye socket. At once Eugene began to shriek, attempting to flail, but the officers and I held strong (though a couple of them began to gag and salivate). Blood spilled thick from the eye and pooled in the crease of my right hand.

"God NOOOOOO!" Eugene screamed. "STOP IT! YUH KILLING MEEEEEEE!!!"

Dr. Freeman drove the pick further into the socket, twisting and screwing it left and right, until it could swing freely. He began to tap the handle to and fro, scrambling the rightmost frontal lobe of Eugene's troubled brain. Gertrude and the young cop holding her both fainted to the floor with two dull thuds. The other cops held on, mouths agape in shock, sweat beading and dripping from their faces.

After five minutes of sloshing the metal spear about in Eugene's brain Dr. Freeman slid the pick out with a moist *sssthwk*. No longer screeching and jerking, Eugene simply twitched, moaning in distant agony.

"*Yessss,*" one of the cops hissed, gritting his teeth in a rapturous grin as Walter began to hammer the pick into the left socket. "*Deeper…deeper…*"

All four officers' eyes shimmered brightly, each becoming ever more excited, their breaths pulsing as one.

By the time Dr. Freeman had finished swinging the pick back and forth within the second eye socket Eugene was no longer moving at all, nor was he making a sound, save his calm, steady breathing. Walter slid the thin spike out of the left eye, and I dabbed up the blood about Eugene's face with a corner of the faded, handmade quilt. A faint smile spread across his lips.

"How do you feel, Mr. O'Dell?" I asked.

"Priddy good…" he slurred, his shut eyelids already beginning to bruise and swell. "Lil sore."

"I can't…believe it," one of the cops said, letting go and wiping his brow. A bright sheen of serene satisfaction radiated from him. "Thought this man was a sure goner. I thought we was gonna hafta—"

"Violence is so seldom necessary," Dr. Freeman said, wiping

the fresh blood from his hands and cleaning the shaft of the ice pick. "Please do remember that."

An ambulance was called. Gertrude was revived, as was the red-haired cop. The Uline was returned to its rightful place. Dr. Freeman and I shook hands.

"Masterful work as always, Doctor," I said.

"All in a day's work, lad," he replied. "All in a day's work."

CHAPTER 2

Dr. Freeman has always called me his assistant, but truth be told, I've never been more than an orderly. Early on he had real assistants on hand. True surgeons and professionals. Dr. Watts, Dr. Lichtenstein, all the various young doctors he trained. But after a while…it was only me. Just ol' Doc and me.

I was working the floors of Poughkeepsie's own Riverside Psychiatric when Doc and I first met. He was already a superstar by then. A super*hero*. We relocated to Washington DC shortly thereafter, a town with which I was already quite familiar. DC would be a good town for superheroes, if any ever bothered to show up.

Everything was right in its place, all right. The trouble with Rosemary…already deep in the past.

"Rosemary Kennedy?" I heard a little voice chirp from the bathroom.

Son of a bitch…there you go thinking out loud again…

She walked into the room proper wearing something just this side of nothing, but for a face full of make-up and a pile of gaudy costume jewelry. She presented herself with a silent *Ta Da!* Swishing about in her short, laced nightie, she began to remove the larger baubles and trinkets from her fingers and ears, and lay them on the lamp table by the bed. Seventeen years old or so if I were guessing, but I never asked. A year younger than yours truly.

"Rosemary Kennedy?" she asked again in that thick, Eastern European accent of hers.

"That'd be the one," I said, taking a deep drink of Johnnie Walker. It ran down my throat like a cool fire, burning and freezing tensions along its path.

"Poor gyul." She picked up the second glass of scotch and sniffed it. "Zis ees for me, yes?"

"It ain't for Red Buttons." I looked about the dingy room, all torn cushions and nicotine stucco. Even more lowdown than normal for me, but I liked it. There's a character to outer-DC motor lodges that you just don't find anywhere else.

"That was Watts' doing anyhow," I continued, "grinding through her skull like that. Traditional lobotomy. *Pshh*. Barbaric horse shit, that's what that is. Thoroughly unnecessary. We don't do that. No ma'am. We go in through the eyes. Trans-orbital is the only way."

"Vot vere you do zere?"

"Huh? Where?"

"Poughkeepsie."

"Oh, you know. The usual." I peeled off my undershirt and lay back on the bed. She settled in beside me, her head on my chest, sapphire nails raking softly up and down my chest. Almost like we were lovers already, but I didn't even know her name yet.

"Sponge baths," I continued, "meal trays…bed pans…hold down the screamers when I gotta. Typical."

"Zot sounds scary and awful."

"It ain't always a humdinger of a hootenanny, that's for damn sure."

"Yoll never scared?"

"Nah."

"Never?"

"Just once," I admitted. "We had this fella…good goddamn. He was something else. More wolverine than man, to tell the truth of it. I thought he was gonna chew right through his leather restraints and rip us all apart with his bare hands. And he could have, no fooling. Salvador Reed was his name. But Doc Freeman and I fixed him right up. He's a teddy bear now."

"My vord."

"It's what we do."

"Ees good vork zot you do."

"Yeah...but before Doc Freeman came along, most of the time I was out back nippin' gin and shootin' dice with the micks. Let me just say, rumors concerning the luck of the Irish have been greatly exaggerated."

"Yoll silly," she giggled.

"Been drifting around this country since I'm knee-high to a grasshopper. I was even slinging pans at Camarillo State when they admitted Bird."

"Who?"

"Charlie Parker. I saw him in his room all by himself. Sweating and shaking. Six months he was there...but I was too yellow to talk to him. Goddamn hospitals...It's all I know. I still have the key to Camarillo."

I downed the rest of my scotch. She attempted to do the same, but coughed and sputtered a bit.

"Careful," I said. She licked her lips and swished the ice in the glass smartly.

"Ees good."

"All that's changed now, though," I said. "We're always on the road these days. On the circuit. In demand. Teaching. Lecturing. Training. Preaching the lobotomy gospel."

"You do lot of ze surgeries still?"

"Do we ever. Sometimes ten a day! Doc Freeman says we'll be doing even more soon. Believe that or not. Psycho-surgery...it's the greatest break-through in medicine since antiseptics...course Doc ain't really too concerned with antiseptics..."

I cleared my throat. She looked at me, puzzled.

"Yeah...Doc and me, we've got our system down," I went on. "Shock 'em, put 'em under, spread the lids, then jab-pop-squish-scramble...and *voila*! Whole new person. A better, happier person. Like that." I snapped my fingers, and found myself growing wistful in spite of myself. And proud. "No more rage. No more fits. No more acting out. You're just…good. For good. Take some time to rest your eyes. And then good forever. Be healed…"

We lay silently, letting the moment settle.

"*Es lamazia*," she said softly. "Zot ees beautiful. Just like Jesus."

"Hey, it ain't me, babe," I said, jumping back to reality. "I'm just the wingman, you understand."

"Yoll Robeen to hees Botmon."

We laughed.

"You're a real doll," I said. "Anybody ever tell you that? You're just like a doll-baby come to life. A satin doll, that's what you are."

"Sank you werry myuch," she said, blushing through a half-inch of rouge. "Yoll not so bad yollsyelf."

"Got any friends you could call on? We could have ourselves a little party here. What do you say?"

"Yoll vant annuzza gyul?"

"Nah, scratch it. We got a nice thing going here. Say doll, where you from anyway?"

"Georgia."

"No foolin'. I met a fellow once from down in Macon. You know Harvey? Runs a little bait shop down there. Lost his leg in the war."

"Vot?"

"Never mind."

"Yoll veird," she said, then grinned coyly. "Cyute, zough."

We clinked glasses.

"Here's to ya," I said.

"*Gaumarjos*."

"Exactly."

"So vot you vant, yeah?"

"Well, well," I said. "Right to the business, eh? OK then. Well, like I said, I want you for the whole night, first of all. I'm

good for it."
"OK. But dyehff'rent fun ees dyehff'rent price."
"Oh yeah?"
"Ees good to haff system in zis line."
"Hey, doll, don't I know it."
"You vant just fuck? OK. Normal price. But to come in my hair? Vill cost. To come on my face? Vill cost. To come on my toes? Vill cost. To come—...vell, you get idea."
"More mess more money. Square deal."
"Yoll vant have my ass? Vill cost MYUCH extra..." Realizing she might be queering the deal with her 'all-business' tone, she suddenly became affectedly flirty again. Nice technique. "But for you ees discount...for cyuteniss."
"Well that's good-a-ya. But here's the thing, honey-kitten. The bottom line. I need you to stay awake. All night. And just watch me."
"Vatch you?"
"You got it. Just watch me."
"Zot's eet?"
"Not too kinky for ya, is it?" I asked. She shrugged. "I don't sleep well, you understand? I spent three of my best years, since I'm fourteen and a half, surrounded...all day every day...by screaming, clawing, jabbering, pants-shitting fruit loops. They threw shit at me, they put voodoo spells on me, they tried to eat my ribcage. It kinda got to me, you know?" I tapped my forehead. "So now, I don't sleep right. And when I do finally drift off, sometimes I stop breathing. For no reason."

I grabbed the bottle from the bedside table, poured myself a shot and guzzled it. She tried to copy me with what was left in her tumbler and choked again on the alcohol.

"Careful now," I said.
"I'm fine, sank you."
"It's...it's like my brain is trying to kill me," I continued. "You know? I'm gonna die in my sleep before I turn twenty-one, and that's no joke. So I can't sleep alone. Least not all the time.

And at least not in DC."

"Vy is DC?"

"I don't know," I said. "It's worse in DC for some reason. But listen, if I stop breathing, or I look distressed in anyway, you gotta wake me up. You get me? Am I coming through clear? You show me I can trust you, and maybe we can work out something long-term. Least when I'm in town."

"I can't do every night! I haff other cyustomers."

"Hey, I hear you. I couldn't afford every night anyhow. Most nights I sleep alone in the Lobotomobile."

"Lobotomobile?"

"That's what Doc Freeman calls the van. Ain't much, but it's home, you know. I take my chances."

She kissed me softly—not a hooker kiss, but a real one.

"You haff sleep now. Vill take care of you. Haff sveet dreams."

"Ain't gonna happen, but thanks all the same, doll."

CHAPTER 3

Pushing the lunch cart at Riverside one fateful day, I heard the voice of Dr. James Watts echo down the corridor.
"You can't do that, Walter!" he said, and I saw him storm out into the hall. He came marching right past me muttering, "Can't take this anymore!"
Just then, Doc Freeman stuck his head out from around a corner.
"You there, lad," he said to me, "can you work a camera?"
How hard can it be? I thought, and headed on down to this cramped little operating room. There he's got a woman, an older dame, unconscious and laid out on her back…with a rubber-handled metal spike jutting straight up out of her right eye socket.
Freeman handed me the camera, watching me to see if I recoil. *I don't.* I didn't know if he was impressed or disappointed that I didn't faint away on sight.
"Get a shot of these angles," he said.
So he knocked the spike back and forth a few times, I clicked off a couple of shots, then he pulled out the rod, sopped up a bit of blood off her face, and woke the dame up. And whatever was ailing her, she's cured…I guess.
And just like that, I was old Doc's right-hand man.
I don't mind living on the road. I've always been pretty much a transient. Working floors from coast to coast, collecting keys

along the way. It's like, every head case I ever encountered, every looney and screwball, infected me with a little piece of his poison. Generous, no? So I kept the keys. I collected them. I kept the keys to the asylums, so I could keep all the crazy hanging right here on my belt loop. And not so much in my head.

Doc and I, we're evangelists, all right. Like the old-time medicine carts…but *for real*. No horse feathers. No snake oil. And through sheer force of will, Doc Freeman made outpatient prefrontal lobotomy the vanguard of psychiatric medicine. After all, the medical community, they're just like everybody else. They wanna be hip. They wanna be with it. They wanna catch the A-train too, don't you know. And who wants to be that one square cat trying to dim a shining star?

CHAPTER 4

Every so often in life you discover something new about yourself. Its significance might not be readily obvious at the time. But you can bet the house on black that it will inform every choice you make from then on. As is often the case with these sorts of revelatory moments in life, it was a day like another other the day I first encountered *chlorpromazine hydrochloride*...

"Good morning, lad."

"Morning, Doctor Freeman."

"I trust you slept well."

"Well enough," I replied, though it wasn't true.

"My apologies," he said, patting his chest in *mea culpa*, "I meant to tell you before, but we're just doing consultations today. You'll not be needed."

"Ah," I said. "Very well then."

I went to make my exit, but noticed a crack in the old Doc's otherwise cool, aristocratic demeanor.

"Everything OK, Walter?" I asked.

"Fine and dandy I don't mind to say," he said.

I nodded, gave a small good-bye salute, and headed for the office door again.

"See ya in the funny pages."

"Say lad," he shouted quickly after me, "have you heard the latest?"

I stopped short.

"Ummm…Not likely, Doc."

"Well…sad news," he said, "seems an associate of mine, Dr. Charlie Stewart…do you remember him?"

"I don't. Sorry."

"Seems Dr. Stewart has just this morning been found dead in his home. Homicide they say…at the hands of a former patient."

"Well damn. Don't that just curdle your morning milk. I'm sorry to hear this."

"Shot in the spine, don't you know."

"Huh. *Déjà vu*, yeah? Just like…when was that you were telling me…'39? Your mentor. Whatsisname…Dr. Moniz."

"Yes," Doc said, clearly surprised that I remembered. "But Egas survived. And recovered. Mostly. No such luck for Dr. Stewart."

"It's a dangerous world, Doc."

"Indeed. And a sick one, to be sure."

"That ain't really what's the matter, though, is it Walter?"

"Well," he snapped, "it has certainly cast a shadow over the day, I'll tell you that." He caught himself, and softened a bit. "The service is this weekend. Somewhere in Maryland. I'm still awaiting details. I don't expect you to attend if you don't wish to."

"I appreciate that," I said. "I've got plans to ball it up a bit this weekend."

"More of that *jazz*, eh?" he replied with a sharp snicker. "I would think you'd want to save yourself a bit for New York next week."

"I'll be ready for the Big Apple, Walter, don't you worry about that."

"Well, it's no matter."

He fidgeted in an uncharacteristically awkward way with various bric-a-brac scattered about his desk.

"Come on, Doc. Spit it out. What's eatin' ya?"

"Oh, it's not much of anything really," he said, waving it off. It was not a convincing performance.

"Uh huh."

"Don't suppose you've heard of this new silliness," he said, forcing a chuckle. "Thorazine is the brand name."

"What-azine?"

"Precisely. Precisely. The 'chemical lobotomy,' they're calling it," he chuckled further, and even less convincingly. "Balderdash."

"You don't say? Chemical lobotomy, huh. You suppose…we're outta business?"

"Certainly not. Ha! The very idea…"

"You sure about that?"

"Utterly," he said. "Nothing but a gauze bandage on a compound fracture if you ask me. If it even works at all. The transorbital lobotomy has no equal."

"Of course."

"1949 is our year, lad. This is the year that it all comes together."

"It's 1950, Doc."

"How's that?"

"It's 1950."

"Oh. Yes, of course. 1950."

"Honest mistake."

"We are blazing new trails here, lad. And nothing will stand in our way. Nothing."

"I have no doubt."

"It would…be good to test it out on a guinea pig, though," he said. "Don't you think? Just to see. Perhaps when we return from the symposium at Columbia, yes?"

"Sure, Doc. Best to dot every i and cross every t, that's what I say."

"Agreed."

More awkward silence, but he seemed relieved to have talked it out, if briefly. I had assumed, given how eager he was to teach others his revolutionary methods and all, that he felt no threat from competition. But then I realized, of course, that the transorbital was *his baby*. He owned it. It was irrevocably tied to him. And this *Thorazine* was an alien presence. It needed to be studied.

And either conquered, or killed.

"Well…" I said finally. "I suppose I'll be moving along then. Let you get to your consultations. Give my best to Marjorie and the kids, and you have a good trip now. My sympathies to whomever and all."

"I will do that," he said, "and I will pass that along."

Walking out the door, I stopped short one last time.

"Say Doc, shot in the dark here, but I thought I might like to borrow a book from you if you don't mind."

"Certainly. Any time. My shelves are yours."

"Thanks a million."

"Something in particular you're looking for?"

"Maybe something on the Eastern Bloc if possible. I don't know. I'm just interested in the region all of the sudden. Maybe a Georgian phrasebook?"

Doc Freeman raised a curious eyebrow.

"Georgian phrasebook?"

"I mean, you know, if you've got one of course."

"I certainly do. But whatever for?"

"For nothing," I said, my face getting hot. "Never mind. I'll see you first thing Monday morning. Take care of yourself, Doc."

"And you as well. Mind yourself, lad. Keep your powder dry and your nose clean. Don't get stuck in a fix."

CHAPTER 5

"*KI!* OH! OH *KI!*" she squealed. "*Menda! Me menda!*"
And so there we were, a spirited, twisted mess of limbs and tangled bed sheets. If she was faking it, it was a superb performance. Had me convinced.
Afterward we lay still, panting and sweating, staring up at the cracked ceiling. We could hear the sounds of like activity emanating through the tissue-thin walls. It was just that kind of a joint.
"Yes," I said, catching my breath, "that'll do. That'll do nicely."
She giggled and clung tightly to me, panting hard.
"Zis job...ees...not so all ze time bad."
"Thanks doll. Right back atcha."
"Vas nice...Vas...werry nice."
We lay in silence for a moment as a couple from across the hall yelled about money.
"So," she continued finally, "not zot eet matters, but my name ees Irina."
"Oh yeah?"
"Uh huh. Irina. Like my muzzah. And hers."
"All right then."
"But you can call me Doll. I like eet."
"Irina. Irina the Satin Doll."
"Es werry nice."

19

"Got a little ring-a-ding to it."

We were silent again for a moment, then she said,

"You don't haff to tell yoll name if yoll not wanting to."

"Maybe someday, doll," I said, stroking her damp, chestnut hair. "My name isn't really so important."

"So…" she said, sitting up, and then, oddly, covering her naked breasts with the bed sheet, "same routine zen? I vatch you tonight so yoll not dying in yoll sleep?"

"I'd sure appreciate it."

"OK. Can I maybe, come morning time, stay in room longer? So I can haff sleep when yoll leaving?"

"You bet. I can get the room 'til later in the day."

She settled comfortably back into the bed with a dreamy sigh.

"*Didi madloba.*"

"You're welcome very much."

She gave me a wry, surprised look.

"No to ze brain cutting zis veekend?" she asked as I got up to pour a couple of drinks.

"We're heading out to New York next week," I said. "Big University. Big symposium. Surgeons, head shrinkers, the whole lot of 'em. I don't really care about any of that shit, though. I just like the town. You ever been? It's not far. Less than five hours by Lobotomobile."

"Not yet, but someday I hope yes."

"Great music. Great vibes. Can't wait. Bird's playing."

"I sink you said he vas in asylum?"

"Not anymore…but he prolly should be."

"Ven I vas leetle gyul, ve live een Moscow foll leetle vhile. Viss my fazzah. My fazzah play jazz music on phonograph record. Before he die."

"You don't say. What was it, do you remember?"

"I sink…Jelly Roll somezing?"

"Jelly Roll Morton."

"Zot's eet! Doctor Jazz Stomp and Big Foot Ham!"

"Yeah, Jelly Roll was great, rest his soul. I was too young to see him, but his records knock me right out. He used to play around here, in DC, not far from where we are right now. 'Til somebody stabbed him."

"Ees dangerous vorld."

"I'll say. So what'd your old man die from?"

"Bullets."

"Yeah, there's a case of that going around."

I handed her a drink. She sipped it lightly.

"I think I need a new home base," I said. "DC is cramping my style."

"Vhere you vant to go?"

"Somewhere exotic. Like…Des Moines, Iowa."

"*Ts'avedit!*"

"You're ready to go now, huh? You coming with me?"

"I'm game foll anyzing, kid."

"Good to know. Good to know."

I wondered how she came about ending up in the good old US of A. What did she do to get here? And why? But then I figured it was probably best that I didn't know. Nothing wrong with a little mystery, after all.

"Say, doll," I said, "you know why they called him 'Jelly Roll?' Jelly Roll Morton?"

"*Ratom?*"

"Eh?"

"Vy?"

"'Cause legend has it," I said, with a dirty grin inching across my mug, "he was packing a big, thick jelly roll in his trousers."

"Mmmmmm, yum yum," she cooed, licking her lips.

We laughed like hell and she kissed me, cuddling close against me.

It must have dawned on both of us at the same time that this was not typical whore & john behavior, and we stopped short. I sat up, wishing the room had a window so I'd have somewhere to look.

"Can I ask vierd question?" she said.

"OK, shoot."

"If somebody hurt you in bad vay, and you sink you could get avay viss eet, do you sink you could kill zot person maybe? Would you haff it in you?"

"Hmmm…Wow. Huh. What a question. I dunno. Could you?"

"Don't know," she said. "Not sure. Perhaps yes. Zis ees just vot I am sinking about sometimes in my head. I haff too much time in my own head. I vish I could not all ze time sink so much."

"Yeah, I know what you mean, doll," I said. "I know what you mean."

And then it hit me like a slap to the kisser.

"Say! That reminds me!" I said.

In a flash I hopped up and headed across the room to my little leather kit bag.

"Vot is?"

"Almost forgot," I said. "I've got myself some homework."

She sat up in bed to watch as I took out a dropper, a syringe, and a thin, solid rubber tube. I tried to handle the goods in a professional, matter-of-fact sort of way…but, sad little secret, I was less than a pro with the needle at that time. I'd been lucky on the job to that point, that when emergency sedatives were needed I was always the brace man, not the jabber. Still, if the need arose, I could load a shot.

"Vot is?" she asked again.

"Not sure, really," I said. "It's called Thorazine. Brand new. Not even on the market yet. Whatever it is, it's got ol' Doc's shorts in a bit of a twist. Said he wanted to try it out on a guinea pig. Well, I'm a go-fer, which is kind of a similar animal."

"How you get if ees not awailable?"

"Facility's got samples on site. I just forged Doc's name on a request form. Ain't the first time."

I loaded the works, and tied off the rubber cord on my left arm. A juicy blue vein popped up ready and willing right away.

"Vot does zis do?"

"I dunno. That's what I gotta find out." I jabbed it straight in on a quick breath. It stung more than it should have. I saw the glass chamber fill with a cloud of my blood, and I pushed the plunger down.

"It's supposed to even you out," I said. "I guess that's right. Makes the demons go away. What about you, baby? You got demons?"

"None of yoll byusiness."

"Yeah, me too. But I'd just as soon get mine drunk, all things being equal." The shit hit my system quicker than I thought it would, and I felt a bit nauseous. My face got soft and spongy for a moment, flush with chemical heat, and I thought I might black out.

"Man alive…"

Then I stabilized. Leveled out.

And suddenly…I was fine. Just fine. I wasn't inebriated. I wasn't floating. It was in no way euphoric. I was simply *fine*. I was just very…very…very slow.

"Last chance, doll," I said, getting ever slower, and more numb. "I don't think I'll be able to do it for you in more than a minute's time."

"I can't haff ugly track marks on my arms," she said nervously. "Ees bad for byusiness."

"Understood. It's a…buyer's market out there."

I watched her mull it over for a moment or two. Then—

Finally, she held up her foot to me.

"No one notice my feet, yes? Can go betveen my toes, yes?"

I tried to smile, but it seemed like needless effort. I felt my expression becoming increasingly flat and slack as I rubbed a vein up on her foot, and injected her. I sat slowly onto the bed.

"There it is…" I said, as well as I could.

"Ooooh…"

"I'm certainly…yeah…"

And we both fell into a mindless stupor.

"*Me…momtsons…es…*"

"Yeah, I like it all right too."

The room appeared to be covered in beige cheesecloth. We sat, completely blank and dazed for what could have been hours. Or seconds. I couldn't really tell.

Finally she turned to me and asked, "Soooooo you vant…Two-foll-von special?"

She slowly climbed on top of me, and we tried to give it another go 'round.

Too listless. Gave up.

"Rain check, satin doll…"

"*Diakhhh…*"

She rolled off of me, and fell fast asleep.

This became a pattern with us. She'd forget to stay awake, I'd forget to pay her. For a time, it worked out OK.

CHAPTER 6

When I think back on the symposium at Columbia University, the abiding memory would have to be standing on the side of the stage in the lecture hall watching Doc Freeman hammer a metal spike into the eye socket of an eerily realistic child-size dummy—
"...So here we simply angle the leucotome, careful to avoid the orb itself, and then forcefully prod the tip directly into the frontal lobe..."
—and looking out into the hall to see the look of horror and nausea on the faces of the assembled medical muckety-mucks.
"*Appalling!*"
"*Outrageous!*"
"*This is thoroughly unacceptable!*"
"*He's not even a proper surgeon!*"
"*Hurumph hurumph!*"
Had it not been for the thin sheen of Thorazine haze coating my system at the moment, I would not have been able to stop myself from cackling like a deranged baboon. It was just so damned funny.
"...And from there," Doc continued casually, "we simply let the instrument swing free, cutting safely through the offending tissue of the rightmost frontal lobe."
A loud outburst of protest rose up from the audience of renowned doctors and neurosurgeons, and some Doctor So-and-so

from *Someplace, Important* just had to stand up and speak.

"Dr. Freeman," Doc So-and-so said, his face ruby red and damp with shock and indignation, "please tell me this is some sort of gag! Your methods, as evident to all in attendance here, are beyond unethical. They are thoroughly, shockingly, bafflingly *reckless.*"

Shouts of agreement popped from the crowd hither and thither. And yon. Doc Freeman just smiled and nodded.

"Thank you, doctor. Your input is most appreciated. Moving on—"

"Dr. Freeman," the interrupter continued, "isn't it true that you have no formal training in surgery whatsoever? And you are, in fact, a neurologist?"

"Sir," said Freeman remaining calm, "I have never professed otherwise. I believe what you will find is so beneficial about the transorbital lobotomy, is the relative ease in which anyone—"

Finally some surgeon from Topeka stood up and shouted—

"To call this man a neurologist is to degrade fine neurologists everywhere! You, sir, are nothing but a dangerous quack, a cheap huckster and a *charlatan*!"

A hearty cheer of affirmation erupted from the crowd, and Doc visibly bristled. He turned to me and said,

"Lad, fetch me *the sack*."

I knew just the sack he meant. We always carried it with us for events such as this, just in case.

I dragged the large burlap bag out onto the stage amidst a chorus of grumbling, shouting and general protest.

"What a sad collection of cowards and philistines have gathered at Columbia University this day," Freeman said, his eyes a-twitch behind scratched, perfectly rounded spectacles. "Allow me to share something with you, gentleman."

He proceeded to up end the sack and dump out the pile of letters and cards contained therein. They scattered all about the floor of the stage in a great and dramatic display.

"Do you see this?" he shouted. "Letters. Postcards. Holiday

greetings. Birthday wishes. From whom? From patients and former patients alike. All of them thanking me. For what you ask? For SAVING THEIR LIVES!"

A deafening hue and cry of sputtering outrage vomited forth from the audience. I stood there dumbly, not really paying much attention.

"Where are your letters, gentlemen?" Doc continued. "Where are your well-wishes? How many people have you actually cured all together? Fifty? One hundred? I have cured THOUSANDS! That is just myself, to say nothing of my numerous students and protégés. And I will cure more poor souls *this month* then the assembled lot of you will in the entire remainder of your careers! This is the vanguard, my friends. Join in or prepare to be left behind."

He turned to me and said, "I'll be in the Lobotomobile. I find this lack of vision tedious."

And with that, he stormed off in a huff, and I proceeded to gather up the letters and stuff them back into the sack. The shouting, angry doctors all exited as well, screaming their impotent outrages as they went.

"Excuse me?" I heard a shaky voice ask from the front of the stage. I looked up to see a tall drink of water with a long, thin face, not but a couple of years older than me standing there awkwardly.

"Hi," he said. "Hello. Hi. How are you? Quite a time today, no?"

"You said it, pal. And you are?"

"Chris Williams," he said, crawling up to the stage proper.

We shook hands, and I continued packing up the test dummy and our demo gear.

"Doctor?" I asked.

"Someday, knock wood."

He looked around, presumably to find some wood to knock on. Finding none (missing the stage itself, apparently), he knocked on his own head.

"Good to know ya," I said, but I cannot honestly say that I was much impressed.

"I'm, uh…I'm looking for Dr. Freeman?"

"He's in the Lobotomobi—he's in the van."

"Um…all right. He's in…? Just sitting there? By himself?"

"That's right," I said. "And buddy, you best not bother him right now. I certainly wouldn't if I were you. Just trust me on that."

"Oh. I see." The young fellow rocked back on his heals nervously for a moment. "I really just wanted to shake his hand and tell him that I am just such a great admirer of his work. And to thank him for all that he's done."

"I see."

"I saw him give a demonstration in San Diego last year. On a live patient. Some of my fellow students actually fainted. Medical students fainting! Can you believe that?"

"Yes I can."

"He's a genius, Dr. Freeman is."

"Uh huh."

"More than a genius. He's a…"

"Go ahead."

"He's a *prophet*. A seer. A healer, the likes of which I did not think actually existed."

"Well, I'll be sure to pass that along."

"He can't let these geezers discourage him. Old know-nothings, the lot of them. They'd still be leeching and bloodletting if they could. Don't they understand that medicine must evolve? It's like an organism. A living organism. New ideas come to life, and replace the old. *Kill them off*. And rightfully so." He paused, looking off into the wings. "And to think, it all started with an ice pick. The humble ice pick."

"Let me ask you something, Chris Williams."

"OK."

"What are your thoughts on Thorazine?"

He scrunched up his forehead, apparently affronted by the very question.

"Nothing but a gauze bandage on a compound fracture," he replied. "The transorbital lobotomy has no equal."

I chuckled. "Gotta love a true believer."

My packing up completed, I began dragging the load from the stage.

"Well, you're a busy man," Chris Williams said. "I'll let you get on with it. Just, please, if you could, let Dr. Freeman know that there are a lot of us out here, ready to follow him into that new frontier. We're with him. We're right behind him. We believe in him."

"Sure thing, pal. You got it."

I may have actually passed it on. Who can remember these things...

Columbia was a bit of a debacle for Doc Freeman. But hey, it's tough being a visionary in your own time. Too bad for him. New York City is always kind to me. That night I saw Bird play...at *Birdland*. Amazing? Stunning? Mystical? Transcendent (whatever that means)? You bet your aunt Fannie's sweet ass. If I believed in God, I'd have to think he'd wanna be at Birdland too just then.

It was a magical joint, Birdland. And I think, even when I'm old and feeble and I don't have but two chipped marbles knocking around inside my coconut, I'll always remember that place.

But that night...I heard something different, something clear that night. Clearer than I had ever heard before. Past the melodies and the chromatic runs. Past the shifting, syncopated rhythms and barely controlled chaos. I heard Parker's turmoil come through in the music that night. The pain...Charlie's pain...goddamn, it was *thick*. The room was humid with it. Like every pitch-bended wail was a cry from his soul. A scream that Parker couldn't actually scream himself. And I thought, *You know, me and Doc Freeman...we could cure that man*. We could make all those tiny devils eating away at him go away. All go away. Hopefully before it's too late.

I opted to not pursue the thought any further, though. For entirely selfish reasons. His pain was my pleasure. You cut that out of Bird, and he's just one more brass honker amidst countless others.

So I decided, once the show was through, to instead just go on back and sleep in the Lobotomobile. And shoot up Thorazine. I stand by that decision. Rooms in New York ain't cheap don't you know. And I'm on a budget.

CHAPTER 7

A few words on Thorazine if I may—
 A full three years before it was even available to the public, I had already developed my habit for the stuff. Notice: *habit*. Not *addiction*. I never craved…much less needed…the way this chemical made me *feel*. Rather, it was because of what I did *not* feel that made it irresistible to me. My habit was not based on what it gave me. I fell in love with it for what it robbed me of.
 Understand; I had never taken myself for a profoundly unhappy person. I lived my life, and what else can you do? But it took my first dose of *chlorpromazine hydrochloride* for me to become acutely aware of a particularly heavy dead sea bird anchored to my neck. In hindsight, it's a wonder I was able to fulfill my assigned duties while weighed down by *empathy*.
 My years, short as they had been at the time, working the institution floors had eaten away great chunks of my *self*, exposing raw nerves in a way that I had never fully recognized, let alone articulated. This was due, in no small part, to the individuals around me then, and how *they* carried *themselves*.
 I was always impressed, if not a bit disturbed, by my fellow staff and crew for what appeared to be their rock-ribbed disregard for the general well-being of our charges (and that's to say nothing of how the doctors regarded them). My heart always secretly ached for those poor wretches we had chained to the walls like rabid

animals, or locked inside padded cells. They hadn't asked for this. They had done nothing wrong to bring this upon themselves…or they had certainly not *chosen* to. It appalled me to see them restrained, often abandoned, and occasionally beaten. And, I loathed having to do the same myself.

But I did it.

I did it every time without a single word of protest.

So I drank instead. I drank to quiet the sound of screams echoing through the corridors from patients strapped down during electrotherapy. I buried that horror deep.

They were sick. They were sick people. They were sick people. But they were never treated as such. They were nothing more than a burden on their families and the state, and I had no doubt that if the state could have gotten away with dumping them all in a large dirt hole and burning them alive they would have gladly done so. I was sure of that. I thought about that a lot. And I drank.

I seldom let on about any of this, of course. I wanted to be a big shot and a tough guy and all, right? And on the rare occasion that I confided in a fellow orderly that I'd like to see the asylums closed someday, he'd invariably just snort and say, "So you wanna be outta work? Go ahead and quit then, chum. I'll take yer hours." So I drank. A lot.

And the screaming kept on well after I left the hospitals behind. Always echoing through the hallways of my skull. And there was nothing I could do to stop it. No action I could take.

But then…like a bolt out of the blue…there was Doctor Walter Freeman. And he told me personally that his singular goal in life was to shut down the goddamned asylums once and for all. To create a world where they would no longer be needed. And the key to that world was the transorbital lobotomy. So simple…so quick…*so permanent*. I swore to stand by him all the way.

But even then the screaming wouldn't stop, until I discovered Thorazine. At last, at last. That did the trick. It quieted the screeching memories. It dulled every jagged edge. It is the perfect cure for *emotion*. And I loved it.

I no longer feared falling asleep, because nightmares have no effect when you are no longer afraid of your own mind. And what difference does sleep paralysis make when your waking self is more or less in a state of mild paralysis anyway?

If only Thorazine didn't wear off. Because when it does, the darkness comes rushing back, and darker than it had been too. You're always going to need more and more. And more. And once you've tasted life without care, without concern, without compassion, reality is far too cumbersome a weight to carry again. The scorching blare of the sun and the bitter, poisoned wind across your brow will destroy you.

And who the hell needs that bullshit?

CHAPTER 8

"Who is the patient, Doctor?"

"Joseph Brinkley. Age twelve. Severe difficulties at home. Possibly schizophrenic. His parents, particularly his stepmother, are at their wits' end. My prognosis: a very serious case of—"

"I…I'm sorry, what?"

"What what?"

"Could you…um…hold on just a minute here, Doc…"

"Which part of that was unclear to you?"

"Did you say the patient is twelve years old?"

"I did, yes. Why? Is there a problem?"

"Uh…Doc, far be it from me to judge your—"

"Yes, far be it from you indeed. What's the matter with you?"

"With all due respect, Dr. Freeman, isn't performing a prefrontal lobotomy on a twelve-year-old boy a tad…extreme?"

"No, it isn't. Not in the least. And I'm troubled by your tone, quite frankly."

"Walter…come on."

"*Come on?*"

"He's twelve years old, for God's sake."

"Yes, he's twelve years old and he is sick and I am his doctor and he is my patient and you are my assistant. Now if no further clarification is required—"

"Walter…you…you are planning to jab an ice pick—"

"I will be using a *leucotome*."

"—into the brain of a twelve-year-old child! Provided he survives—"

"Provided he survives? Provided he *survives*?! He will survive, of course, and he will be cured. Of course. Are you…having doubts about our work?"

"Of course not. It's just—"

"Do you agree that the lobotomy is medicine?"

"What?"

"DO YOU AGREE that the lobotomy is medicine?"

"Of course I do. Don't be ridic—"

"Of course you do. Because if you did not, that would make you a monster. A butcher. Or at least an accomplice to butchery. And that would be an unthinkable thought to ponder at this point, would it not, Lad?"

"I don't think…I mean, I don't doubt—"

"If we are in agreement that the lobotomy is indeed medicine, as I'm sure we all are, then is it not IMMORAL, besides being a violation of my oath as a doctor, to deny a sick child the treatment that he so desperately requires?"

"It…it is. Yes."

"Make the preparations. Joseph and his parents are on their way. And make sure the camera has film. We will be remembered for this one."

CHAPTER 9

Joseph Brinkley was a pudgy little so-and-so, and a great heap of a kid to be sure. Even knocked out cold he had something of a punk's look about him, his gaping mouth like a silent, full-throated holler. It was a cinch to picture this kid giving his folks a hard way to go. Reminded me of some of the dirty fink bastards from back at the orphanage, the guys who would trap sewer rats in cardboard boxes in the back alley and then set them on fire. The type who grew up to join biker gangs, or the police force. Probably a real bite in the ass to every person who had to deal with him. And it bothered me.

We did him right there in the office as his stepmom sat outside filing her peach painted fingernails. They matched her dress perfectly.

"We'll be done in two shakes, Mrs. Brinkley," I said with a big smile spread across my face as I headed toward the office with the camera. "Don't you worry about a thing."

"You just fix him good," is all she said to me, never bothering to look up from her nails.

I decided to be clean for this one, and I don't know why. Of all the days to dull my senses, this would have been a good one. And as I started snapping shots, careful to keep the orbs in focus as Doc sloshed and squished about the kid's brain with his spike, chuckling quietly to himself, I thought about how much better

that boy's life would be after he was fixed. What delightful company he would be. What an easy, affable presence he would now be in his home, and within the society at large. And as I stood there watching Doc Freeman tap the hammer and work his magic, I couldn't help but think that that boy's blank, glassy, bleeding eyes would never shimmer with life in them ever again. Never flash with a mischievous impulse or burn with rage. And it bothered me.
    And it bothered me.
    And it bothered me.
    And it bothered me.

CHAPTER 10

I sat on the corner of the bed, gulping from my tumbler of dark rum. She lay across the bed in her milk-white slip, blank and serene.

"Vot I love about zis Thorazine?" she cooed lazily, "Ees not a high. Ees no high at oll…" She still needed me to shoot her up, not ready to work the needle herself, which was just as well. "Ees…just…nice and empty…"

It's good to be needed after all.

"Too young…" I whispered to myself. "He was too young…"

I downed the glass, and it burned my chest cavity like flaming gasoline.

"Vonderfully empty…"

I thought for a moment that I was not in an acceptable mindset that night to dose myself with any medicine stronger than liquor. But I wanted this feeling of grime and filth gone from me. And I knew that I couldn't scrub it off.

I picked up the dropper and needle from the bedside table. I loaded the syringe and saw the bubbles dancing inside. No matter. It was not going in the vein.

"Like vaking dreamless sleep…"

"Too young…just too damn young…"

"Never vant to sink again…"

I shot it into the back muscle of my left tricep. Still too much pinch. It made a squishing sound as I pressed the plunger in.

"*Nous avons foi au poison...*"
I looked back at her as my mouth filled with cotton, and my face turned to sponge. I could see her, but I felt myself losing the incentive to focus.
"Didn't know you spoke French, doll."
"I don't," she whispered. "I speak *Rimbaud*."
"Well I'll be."
"Hollow..." she sang to herself, fond of the sound, and the feel of the word in her mouth, I suppose. "Hollow hollow hollow..."
I lay down on the bed in what little room she had left for me. Curled on my right side, I was careful to keep my left arm up, as it was still tender. Putting the juice in my muscle instead of the vein would help it slide into my system more quickly. Or so I read. I hoped it would settle in as I fell asleep. The last thing I heard as I drifted off was Irina the Georgian whore half-singing, half-whispering—
"Hollow...Hollow...Hooollloooooooowwwww..."

Black nothing. And awake. Paralyzed. And suffocating. I force my eyelids open to mere slits, and I see her, still laying across the bed, singing to herself. Fingers dancing lightly in the air like floating feather lint. My mouth gapes and I desperately try to breathe. No air. I scream. No sound. I scream to her, Wake me up! WAKE ME UP!!! Nothing. Only my eyes can move. IRINA PLEASE! I strain my eyes into their corners, pushing hard, hoping the pain in the muscles will be enough to shock my body awake. Nothing. WAAAAAKE MEEEE UUUUUUUUUUUUUUUP!!! She does not notice me. Oblivious. And hollow. I suck in a pinch of air...just enough to keep myself alive for the moment...I'm dying...I am dying...
Irina...wake...me...up...Irina...please...wake...wake...me...wake me...wake me...up...

* * *

Suddenly I jerked awake, thrashing about, dragging in great gulps of new air.

"AAAAAAAAAAAAAAAAAAAAAAAAAAAAAHHHH!!!"

She screamed and fell from the bed with a thud.

"VOT IS?! VOT IS?!"

"Dying…" I gasped. "Screaming inside…my head…Wake up! Wake me up! You…you're supposed to wake me up!"

"Vot is matter vis you!?!?" she shrieked.

"I told you…to wake me up…if I look like I'm in trouble!"

"I can hardly just move!" she screeched at me, flailing her arms about, lost and disoriented. "Yoll idea!" she screamed. "Yoll idea to shoot me up!"

Her hysterics were disproportionate to my relative anger. I was actually more relieved to be alive than I was mad at her. But she was beside herself.

She began to sob, "I vant j-j-just fuck like normal trick! Ees no trah'ble! Zot ees vot I do!—*sob*- YOU give me Thorazine! L-Look! Look at my feet!" she screamed, attempting to life a foot and stumbling. "Holes in my feet LIKE JESUS!—*sob*- You do! YOU DO to me! Zis vas yoll idea!"

"My idea was to live, dollface," I said, finally catching my breath. "What am I paying you for after all?"

Wrong thing to say. Her face contorted in rage.

"YOLL BARELY PAYING ME!!!"

She grabbed her clothes off the floor and stumbled from the room, sobbing. She left her shoes behind. Guess I could have kept them, Cinderella-style, but I didn't.

Her word rang in my head long after she had gone. Her words, but they were my voice. *Your idea…this was your idea…*

I was too discombobulated to stand, and remained on the bed tangled in sheets, still gasping for air.

After a while, I was sure I saw a figure standing at the foot of my bed, but I couldn't make it out. Nothing but a dark silhouette.

"Hello, lad," Dr. Freeman said, muffled and distant as if through a tin horn. "Rest well, did we? I hate to always be the harbinger of ill tidings, but do you remember a Dr. Showalter of San Diego? It's been a year at least, so perhaps you don't."

He stepped forward, and into focus. Slight man though he was, it felt as if he were towering over me.

"Seems he has fallen to his death from a third-story window," he continued. "They're not ruling out suicide. I didn't know him so well, but still and all…It's a loss I'm sure."

"I'm sure."

"So…I'm eager to hear of your findings."

"What findings would those be, Doc?"

"You've been testing the new chemical. I know you've been scripting it yourself. I'd be bothered, of course, under normal circumstances. We could both be neck deep in hot soup if someone were to find this out. But I know you're working for the greater good. I admire your renegade spirit, quite frankly."

"The study's a failure, Doc. See? I've got no control case. It's just me and the juice."

"Hmm. Well, tell me how you feel at least. Have you achieved some peace of mind?"

"Do I look at peace to you, Walter?"

"Alas. Perhaps then you should just come off the stuff now."

A jolt of terror and nausea shot through me at the thought of kicking.

"NO," I said, trying to shout, but failing. "Not a chance. I'm not coming off. I'm *never* coming off. It makes the world fuzzy and dull. Softer. Less sharp. Less of a hideous, jagged, stinking waste pit. It helps me not to care."

"Oh come now."

"Life is a mistake, Walter. A stupid, random, pointless mistake. A bad cosmic joke. Anything that blocks it out is a damn good thing I say. They ought to dump this shit in every box of Cracker Jacks."

"I see. Very interesting hypothesis."

"You shouldn't have done the child, Doc. You shouldn't have done it. *We* shouldn't have done it. We shouldn't have carved up his brain. He was only twelve years old, Doc. His brain was still growing. How can you cut a brain that still needs to grow?"

"He was sick," he said. "They were all sick. And now they're all better. Now the world they live in is that soft, rounded place you yourself will not relinquish. Only difference is…their new soft world is *permanent*. Yours is always a needle away. Yes? You know the pain and the madness, lad, it cannot be talked away, can it. Freud can take a hike, am I right? Right off the long pier. And it can't be drunk away. Not with liquor. If anything, that makes it worse. Doesn't it, lad. No, it needs to be cut out. Slashed and scrambled. The world needs a lobotomy, lad. You know that even better than I. I've come to bring peace to the world. Inner peace. Peace of mind. And I hope that you'll continue to assist me. We are doing well, and we are doing *good*. *For good*."

"So what's next, Walter? What's the next step from here? Where do we go now?"

"So glad you asked. We are booked for a two-week stint in West Virginia at the beginning of July. Two hundred and eighty-eight transorbital lobotomies in fourteen days. Imagine that. They're calling it 'Operation: Ice Pick.' Isn't that just grand?"

"It's a hoot and a holler, Doc."

"Come save the world with me, Lad. I'm eager to show you my new technique. Here soon I plan to *double my productivity*."

He smiled, and pulled out two leucotomes, one for each hand. Doc Freeman walked behind a white curtain I hadn't noticed was there and pulled out a gurney with some patient strapped down to it. Gagged, awake, struggling, and terrified. Desperate. Pleading eyes clamped open. I didn't recognize the patient. He was strange to me.

"There there, Ralph, just relax," Doc Freeman said, and quick as a wink, plunged both ice picks into both of the man's eyes at the same time. I could only watch slack-jawed and numb as Freeman cackled madly to himself, furiously hammering both of the picks deeper and deeper into the poor sap's head.

And then it all went black again.

I woke some hours later in that same motor lodge, in that same dingy room, still tangled in those same ratty sheets, relieved to discover that it had been a dream. Except that it hadn't been a dream at all. It was a memory. Ralph Benton was cured by a two-fisted transorbital lobotomy on August 12, 1954. I must have been there. I have the photographs.

CHAPTER 11

The transorbital lobotomy, ever more by the day, became Doctor Freeman's abiding obsession. Like an addiction. The pair of us traveled the country non-stop, performing as many as possible…almost as if old Doc knew his time as a lobotomist was coming to an end.

Another symposium in San Francisco nearly erupted in chaos when Doc brought out then fourteen-year-old Joseph Brinkley as proof of the procedure's safety and success. I barely remember this. I was drunk. I may have actually been asleep at the time. I do remember that Joseph was no small fry by then. Nearly six feet tall, and thick. He refused to speak, or make eye contact. His head was always down, black hair hung like a little curtain over his forehead, shielding his eyes, and if it had been longer he would have worn it like a mask. But, he was calm. He was obedient. He was quiet. He was *good* now. He was a success.

As time ticked by, I was less and less convinced of the rightness of the procedure. So, in keeping with the way I tend to conduct my business, I numbed myself. I numbed my guilt with alcohol and Thorazine. I never had the guts to protest again, and I just blinded myself instead. It did not go unnoticed.

"Your behavior, Lad, is becoming increasingly erratic. Do shape up."

The final straw? When Doc Freeman decided to perform a prefrontal lobotomy on an eight-year-old girl (and then he went younger still). That was it for me. When he set up an office in California, I did not go with him. I walked out on him. And I didn't look back. I've always been partial to the East anyway, and I'm certainly not the Sunnyvale sort.

And it was then that things started to go very, very wrong.

People started dying. Old patients, early subjects, began suffering massive hemorrhages.

And then shortly thereafter, the suicides began. The dead piled up.

It was just a few at first, but they piled up. More and more. Higher and higher. Some people, it seems, just don't take too comfortably to the prefrontal lobotomy.

And even still…no one talked about it. It was seldom, if ever, discussed. It was as if, you know, oh well, *these things happen*. Medicine is not an exact science after all. If we start holding doctors accountable for every little misstep, they'll become too timid and gun-shy to work at all. And where would that get us in the end?

Understand, though, Doc Freeman loved his patients. Don't get me wrong. He loved them one and all. And even after the procedure fell out of favor, and even Doc himself mostly stopped doing them, he continued to travel the country coast to coast, making home visits. Checking on progress. Convincing himself that the results, whatever they were, affirmed the rightness of his technique.

Three thousand, five hundred lobotomies, give or take. That's how many he did himself. Some with me, many without. Eighteen thousand transorbitals all told when you factor in the work of his students and protégés. That's a helluva lotta scrambled gray matter. An awful lot of people who would never be the same. People who would never think or feel or communicate as they once had.

Doc was certainly convinced…still convinced it was all good and proper medicine. Maybe he was right. He was THE expert after all…and his own greatest disciple.

As for me? I had to ramble too. Keep moving. I went back to the asylums. Pushing carts, dumping pans. Of course I did. It's what I do. It is what I have always done.

Somewhere along the grapevine I heard that one of Freeman's protégés has been found dead of an apparent homicide. Attempted robbery, or something. Street mugging.

And then another.

And another.

I couldn't be concerned, though. Why would I be concerned? I was too busy…self-administering my own lobotomy. Who am I to try and figure these things after all?

Who am I?

Who *am* I?

One night, in New York, in the year of our Lord nineteen hundred and fifty-five, in a smoky little Bowery dive, I saw Bird play for the last time. And I once again passed up the chance to talk to him, to meet him, even to just thank him for his music.

That night both of us would go to our respective hotel rooms—he at The Stanhope, me somewhere cheaper—and shoot up. Only one of us would ever see the sun shine again. And not the one of us the world actually needed.

PART TWO
THE TRANSORBITALS
CHAPTER 12

1968, baby, all right? Outta sight. Thirteen years…OK…thirteen years…

But you know me; I just did my thing. Pushing carts, working the floors. Couldn't stick to one place for too long. Always some new institution somewhere, always a brand-new key to add to the chain.

I'd kept myself out of trouble, though, for the most part. Did a little time in '59 over a bar fight, but no real harm done.

Kept a switchblade, a buck knife, and a blackjack on my utility belt. Lost count of all the dark figures who lurched on me from the alleyways. I'd Slash and stab my way out of it, and never seem to catch a face. Not so much as a glimpse. They'd all run off before I could. But that's life, right? Sure it is.

Of course, I could never be certain if they were really there or not. The eyes, the brain, they're tricky vessels to be sure. I don't trust anyone else's, and I have no real cause to trust mine either.

One thing I will say for that Vietnam they've got going on:

good for business where I come from. Job security. Every other day yields a fresh batch of new patients. *Hey hey, LBJ, you break another kid? Just send him our way!*

No concern of mine. *Just do the job, pay the bills, make sure wherever you are, you've got a key to the medicine box.* Thorazine's there to keep me right and steady, and no harm done. No harm done.

Couldn't help but think back, though…sometimes…here and there…couldn't help but think back on a time when I felt like we were really doing something. When we were really making a difference. Side by side with a superhero. That was sure something all right.

But hey, at least it was good to be back at Riverside again.

CHAPTER 13

"Excuse me! You there, orderly!"
I could work Riverside sleepwalking.
"Over here!"
I know those floors like I know old St. Joseph's Orphanage where I grew up...
"Hello there?"
...Maybe better even. As such, I tended to switch into autopilot during my rounds.
"I could really use your help with...*You*!"
"Me?"
I turned around to find a flustered, younger doctor trotting down the corridor toward me, his long, thin face red and sweaty. I thought I recognized him, but wasn't entirely sure. Nor was I in any way interested.
"It's you!" he said, huffing and puffing up to me.
"Are you sure?"
"It IS you!"
"Nah."
He approached as if he had made some sort of grand discovery.
"Oh my God," he exclaimed. "How have you be—...I've only just started here at Riverside...It's been, what, almost twenty years. Do you remember me?"
"No, doctor."

"The symposium?"
"That doesn't really help, doctor."
"Columbia University? When was that, '51? '52?"
"Well..."
"I'm Chris Williams. Remember?"
"Ah, yes. How you doing there, Doctor Williams?"
"OK," he said, "all things considered. I've only just started here."
"You don't say."
"Now how is this for serendipity?" he said, smiling brightly and wiping his forearm across his brow.
"I'm not sure...how is it?"
"You know, I'm not really one for 'fate' or any of that rot, but damn it all..."
And so there we stood, blocking foot traffic both ways, rubber soles squeaking around us on both sides.
"Umm, did you need me for something, Dr. Williams?"
"As a matter of fact..." He looked suspiciously around the hallway, then leaned in and whispered conspiratorially, "*Yes I do.*"
Though his attention was flattering, he was beginning to creep me out a bit—
"Food tray?" I asked. "Medicine? Problem with a screamer?"
—and besides, I had work to do.
"No no no!" he replied. "Well, yes. But...we'll get someone else to handle that. Right now, I need YOUR help. And *only yours*." He looked around again and then whispered even more quietly than before, "*And you mustn't breathe a word of it. To anyone. Do you understand?*"
"Not a word of it."
"Follow me. I need to show you something."
We headed up to the third floor to his cramped, drab little office; papers, coffee cups and various brik-a-brak sat stacked on his desk and each of the two available chairs. For a doctor he struck me as tremendously disorganized, and unnervingly distracted. It occurred to me that perhaps this fellow had chosen the wrong

line of work.

"All right...let's see here...No...no, this isn't it..."

He rifled through two separate briefcases, finally pulling out several neatly collated stacks of papers from each.

Perhaps it was less that he was disorganized...but rather his priorities were oddly focused.

"Some...uh...secret project you got going there, Doc?"

"You could say that," he said, nodding gravely. "Yes. You could indeed put it that way. If...you consider life itself to be merely a project."

"As a matter of fact I do."

"Mistakes have been made, my friend. Mistakes have been made."

"Um. Sure."

"We no longer speak of the transorbital lobotomy, you know."

"Yes," I said. "That appears to be the way of things these days."

"It really did seem like a break-through at one time," he said with a sigh. He plopped down on the tan leather couch, the only free sitting area, and indicated that I should sit as well.

"I know," I said, sitting on the opposite end of the couch. "It did at that."

"Didn't it? Didn't it seem that way?"

"I suppose."

"Everyone makes mistakes. We're only human, after all. The science is not precise."

I couldn't help but laugh at this, and I'm not sure why. "You say so, Doc."

"Tell me, friend," he said, "when have you last seen Dr. Freeman?"

"Oh...Jesus. Thirteen years? At least that."

"Damn," he said, giving the armrest of the couch a light thump. "I feared as much."

"What's this about, Doctor Williams?"

"Call me Chris."

"OK."

"Take a gander at these, will you?"

He handed me several sheets of loose paper. It was a list of names, last name first, followed by a series of dates. Most of them contained an accompanying MD.

"Do you recognize them?" he asked. "Any of them?"

"Maybe," I said. A few did ring a tiny bell in my head somewhere. "Yeah, maybe. I think they were…protégés of Dr. Freeman? Some of them anyway. Many blue moons ago."

"Yes!" he said brightly. "Yes, exactly. But that's not all they have in common."

"Uh huh?"

"They're also…all dead now. Every single mother-loving last one of them."

"Oh…oh yeah?"

"You seem…unfazed by this."

"Well, you know, eggs in China…"

"You don't find anything disturbing about so many doctors turning up dead? And at such relatively young ages to boot?" My blank look continued unabated. "With this *common trait* binding them together?"

Been doing a bit of detective work, have we Doc? I don't know if that's the proper uniform for a gumshoe." I laughed. He did not. "I'm just sayin' is all."

He straightened his back and cleared his throat.

"These cannot be mere coincidence," he said, emphatically tapping the papers with his index finger. "Someone is out there—!" He lowered his voice, "Someone is out there…*killing doctors*. But not just doctors. *Lobotomists*."

"Oh."

"Oh? I say there's a killer on the loose and you have nothing to say but 'Oh'?"

"Well…OK. How's this…*Eighteen thousand*."

"Sorry?"

"Eighteen thousand. That's how many prefrontal lobotomies have been performed over the last 20 years. Mostly through the previous decade. Now, Doc Freeman himself is responsible for nearly four thousand of those. I know, 'cause I was there for a good chunk of them. But, that still leaves a whole heaping helping of folks working the scene. Laying down that routine. All right? He trained a LOT of people. A lot. And now you're telling me, over the past two decades or so, that a handful of them, from all over the country, have passed away? Some from…" I flipped to a corresponding page listing causes of death, "accidents around the office…'natural causes'…a couple of suicides…and so on. Is that what's spooking ya, Doc? That sounds to me like life doing what it does. No need to call out Sam Spade, OK? Or the National Guard or something."

He studied me stiff-lipped for a long moment.

"Oh," he said in a clipped tone. "I see."

"Well…good."

"Fair enough," he said, a thin smile barely cracking his angular face. "I hear what you're saying."

"It's just how things look from where I'm sitting," I said.

"I'm glad you mentioned the eighteen hundred."

"Thousand."

"What?"

"Eighteen thousand prefrontal lobotomies. In two decades."

"Yes. Of course. Eighteen thousand. So have you kept up with any of them?"

"What? Of course not. I mean, not really. Just a few."

"Well," he said, his cryptic grin now spreading wider. "Walter Freeman has."

"Yes. I know."

"He travels the country in that old…*Lobotomobile* of yours, the camper van, constantly checking in on former patients. Almost pathological really."

"That sounds like Walter all right."

"I've begun keeping up on them too," he said. "All of the out-patient prefrontals. Or many of them anyway. The range of reaction from this procedure is…*staggering*. There is no consistency at all. AT ALL. Some of them are actually what one might charitably call 'cured.' No more rage, no more fits, relatively peaceful and productive citizens."

"But…" I sighed, as a familiar sinking feeling came over me.

"But…not very many of them." He handed me a thicker stack of papers. "Do you recognize *these* names?"

I did. And I felt my stomach fall.

"Yes," I answered more quietly than I meant to. "Yes I do."

"Former patients?"

"Yeah."

"How many of them do you guess are all better now?"

I began to feel the sweat break on my forehead. I felt myself getting shaky and agitated, I began to *actually feel*, and I had a strong urge to run off to the medicine closet for a moment or two.

"Um…Most of them?" I said with a weak smile.

"Nice try," he said. "If only Rosemary Kennedy had been an unfortunate oddity. If anything, that old girl got off easy, comparatively speaking."

The shame and guilt must have begun dripping from my face.

"Rosemary wasn't a transorbital," I said. "And she was before my time…it was Dr. Watt's, you know. His fault."

"Uh huh," he said, nodding in faux agreement. "Well that's just super-duper. And so is that what's going to help you sleep at night?"

I chuckled. "Get outta my head, you bastard."

"Hey, don't blame yourself," he said, "I did it too! *We all did it*. It seemed like the magic bullet. Right?"

"Yeah…"

"We could finally close down these wretched institutions. No more shock. No more drugs. We could heal the world, am I right about this? Am I speaking out of school here? Isn't that what *we all* thought?"

"I think so…"

"But that's not what happened, friend. No sir. That is not what happened at all. Every cut of the ice pick was like a coin-flip on someone's life. No...it wasn't a coin flip. It was a spin of the roulette wheel." *Déjà vu.* "For every one true success, we'd have ten fall into a full vegetative state. Or revert to infantilism. Or develop horrific physical and vocal tics. Spasms. Loss of motor control. Loss of bladder and bowel control. Tardive dyskinesia. And some just...went blank. And that's to say nothing of the massive brain hemorrhaging."

"To say nothing at all."

"And death. God, so many deaths. It's amazing we haven't all been carted away in chains."

"Doctors don't get punished for bad medicine."

"Not yet. Or perhaps, not officially."

"I really don't...want to care about any of this," I said awkwardly. And I really didn't.

"But you *do* care," he said. "Am I wrong? Tell me if I am."

I didn't want to talk about this anymore. A needle was whispering my name somewhere. Calling me back to the land of oblivion.

"So..." I said, trying to focus hard on the discussion at hand, "you believe there's a killer on the loose."

"That's my working hypothesis at the moment."

"With a vendetta of some sort."

"Not necessarily."

"You think it's, what, a rogue doctor?" He didn't answer, but his silence said 'perhaps.'

"Suspects?"

"None yet."

"OK," I said. "OK. So...if someone is really out there knocking off lobotomists...there is kind of a big white gorilla in the room here, wouldn't you say?"

He looked at me quizzically.

"All right?" he said.

"Why is Doc Freeman still walking around fine and dandy?" He arched his right eyebrow, but didn't reply. "A bit of a hole in your theory...isn't it, Chris? Huh? Isn't it?"

"There's more," he said, leaning in. "And before you ask, yes,

I have spoken to the police about this. On several occasions. And they are clearly not making connections for the very reasons you mentioned: all these dead lobotomists, seventeen at last count, from all different parts of the country, and spread over at least a fifteen-year period…if not longer…it just seems random and coincidental. Eh?"

"It does indeed."

"BUT! That just shows what a crafty…!" he stopped short, then redirected. "And the police are incapable of connecting…or unwilling to connect…the obvious dots."

I found his intensity more than a bit disconcerting. But, I worried more that he might in fact have been on to something.

"Uh, Chris—"

"Thanks to Doctor Freeman's legendary affinity for self-promotion," he said, rifling through the papers again in search of the appropriate documents, "it has not been difficult to trace his travel routes going back many years…"

"And?"

"And what I've discovered is…over the last seven and a half of those years, a number of these so-called 'random' and/or accidental deaths have taken place…*when Freeman was in the vicinity.*"

I found myself bristling at what I assumed was his implication here. My reaction surprised me. But I could not help but feel defensive of Doc Freeman.

"Now come on…surely you don't mean to—"

"All I'm saying is," he said quickly, "that it sounds like a connection to me. And you say, 'But Chris, somebody's bumping off lobotomists, then why doesn't that somebody take out the king fish?'"

"The 'king fish?'"

"The big kahuna, the head cheese…"

"Right."

"Well…I don't know," he said with a grand shrug. "I don't have an answer. I don't have ANY answers. Yet. But whomever it is, they certainly seem to be following his shadow."

"If this person even exits."

"Yes. Exactly."

"OK," I said. "Let's pause for a moment of perspective, shall we?"

"Sure."

"None of this changes the fact that several of these doctors died of fucking *heart attacks*, for godsake! And cancer!"

"And some of them didn't!"

"One of them fell down a flight of stairs at his daughter's birthday party!" I shouted back.

"Look," he said, regaining his composure. I did likewise, but I really wanted to leave. I needed to tend to my rounds. "Maybe they're not all connected...but what if even *some of them* are?"

"What difference would it make?" I said.

"The last two," he said, "the most recent, they scare me most of all. Dr. Kirk Vollman, April of last year. And Dr. Bruce Haines, *three weeks ago*. Kirk Vollman was found in an alley outside his office in St. Paul, Minnesota with his head caved in and his wallet stolen."

"Sounds like a mugging to me."

"Bruce Haines was found dead in his apartment in Washington DC. Stabbed repeatedly in the face. Heavy stab wounds to and around *his eyes*. Nothing in the apartment stolen."

"And you think...what, that this is a message of some sort?"

"Do you recognize this name?" he asked. "Bruce Haines?"

"Not really."

"That's because Bruce Haines was not a protégé of Freeman's. He attended exactly one guest lecture. San Diego, 1950. I know, because I was there too. Bruce Haines was a classmate of mine in med school. He was only a practicing physician for four years before quitting and going into business with his brother selling surgical equipment and ER supplies.

"Now," he continued, "perhaps I'm just a total loony tune, and I pray that I am. But if I'm not, and Bruce Haines was hunted down and murdered...for his brief time as a lobotomist...then

I'm likely being hunted too. And…*so are you.*"

All of the sudden, the occasional random attack by muggers and street people didn't feel so random, or occasional, anymore.

"But look, man," I said, still trying to keep the burden of this away from me, "all these people…they're ALL *doctors*. Or people who were doctors at one point. I'm not a doctor. And I never have been."

"That's true," he said with a nod. "And you think that's going to keep you safe?"

"I can take care of myself," I said, almost convincingly. "I've seen my share of bad shit out there, Chris, and I've made it this far."

"Well…" he said, "Suit yourself. You could just walk away. Hope for the best, right? Good luck and godspeed and all of that."

"But…you know I won't do that."

"I don't know that for sure. But I do hope."

"You're really scared, aren't you," I said. "I mean you genuinely are afraid."

"That is part of it, I won't lie," he replied. "But you have to understand…I didn't get into this line of work because I craved fortune. Or fame."

"Unlike some people we know?" I said.

"I truly wanted to help people," he continued. "To heal. I honestly thought, in my own small, personal way, I could do my part to…you know…*save the world*. That's sounds stupid to you, I'm sure."

"Not as stupid as it should," I said.

"*Do no harm.* That's the vow we all take. First, do no harm. It's not official, but it is solemn. At least to me. Not only do I feel that I may have failed as a healer, I may have failed in my vow as well. I can't stand idly by and allow even more harm to happen without trying to stop it. Does that makes sense to you at all?"

"Yes. It does."

"Freeman is the connection to it all," he said carefully. "You knew him better than anyone. Better than his own wife, probably. I need your help, my friend. I need your help."

CHAPTER 14

Dr. Williams and I began to see quite a bit of each other. At work and after. He had apparently tried to talk to others about his fears and theories in the hopes of garnering some interest into an investigation of some sort, but he was soundly rebuffed across the board. Not wanting to look like he had flipped the proverbial lid (a fairly common occurrence with brain doctors, as you might imagine), he generally tried to shut his face about it, and I think he was grateful that I was at least marginally open to what he had to say. So he latched onto me as something of a kindred.

His wife had recently walked out on him as well, fed up as she apparently was with the twitchy, miserable bastard Riverside had turned him into.

Dumb luck, that.

I could certainly empathize with all parties on that front. You'd have to be a ghoulish son of a bitch to not have the wards affect you, and Riverside was actually a pretty decent facility comparatively speaking. But with his wife and their two young daughters gone, he had an inordinate amount of time to stew on this issue.

"You know," Chris said one night as we drank malted scotch on the patio of his old Duchess County farmhouse, "I was always very careful. I took great pains to only sever the white fibers connected to the thalamus. This notion of 'scrambling' the frontal lobes never made much sense to me. I only severed the white fibers. That's it."

"Well good for you," I said sipping heartily at my drink, enjoying the fine vintage Chris's salary afforded him. "You're one of the few."

"Even using an experimental treatment, it is imperative to exercise the utmost care and caution. I've said that since day one."

"So you always sterilized your hands and instruments before surgery?" I asked.

"What?!" he spat, nearly choking, "Of COURSE I did! What sort of a crazy question is that?! What kind of doctor doesn't sterilize before surgery?"

"You'd be surprised," I said with a shrug. "You would be surprised."

"I just keep thinking about Egas Moniz," he said, pouring himself another drink. "It may be nothing, but he's been on my mind a lot recently."

"Because one of his own patients attacked him?"

"Mostly."

"You think it's a patient?"

"I'm just thinking out loud."

"Pretty unlikely," I said, trying to plot the right time to excuse myself for a moment. I never officially announced my Thorazine habit to Chris, but I didn't exactly work too hard to keep it from him either. The need wasn't urgent just yet, so I decided to play it cool for the time being. It's all about pacing. And to be sure, my conversational skills were bound to take a nosedive once I got it in the vein.

"If what you think is actually going down *is*," I said, "there is no way even the most high-functioning lobotomy patient would be able to pull this off in secret, for this amount of time, over such a large stretch of geography. It's kind of the nature of the operation that this sort of thing can't happen. You know?"

"True enough," he said, "but there is the Mary Watson situation to consider."

Dr. Marshall Tannen of Tulsa, Oklahoma, was one of the

seventeen. On June 3, 1964 he was found dead in his car, stabbed repeatedly in his chest with what forensic specialists claimed was likely a serrated hunting knife. His wallet and wedding band were taken, as was a very expensive leather briefcase. Not long after news of the crime hit the papers a former patient of his, Mary Watson, came forth and confessed to the murder. After she confessed, her nephew and his wife who Mary lived with at the time claimed that, at the estimated time of the killing Mary was in their dining room, seventy miles away, working on a puzzle. Their story was backed up not only by their children, but several neighbors who were visiting at the time.

"Mary Watson proves my point exactly," I said. "When she was asked what she used to kill Dr. Tannen with, the old girl brought out a pair of plastic salad tongs."

"Right," Chris said, "Of course. But what I'm saying is; a patient, under the suggestion of a trusted, charismatic—"

"Come on, Doc," I said, I said with a sigh. I knew where he was going with this.

"Let's say someone, someone the patient trusted, someone who could easily influence them—"

"Someone like Dr. Freeman maybe? That's what you're getting at. Why would he do that? What could his motivation possibly be for having his former students killed?"

"What is Freeman's motivation for *anything* he does?"

"To heal," I said. "That's his motivation." I wanted to believe that. It sounded as far from convincing as it felt.

"The transorbital lobotomy has lost its respectability over the last few years," said Chris. "And so has he. Maybe he blames them for souring his shiny apple." I thought it interesting that he said *them* instead of *us*. "I don't know. Like I said, I'm just thinking out loud here. But it is suspicious how *physically nearby* he has been when so many of the deaths occurred. And…let's be honest, he's not long for this world. His health is deteriorating rapidly. If there were any chance left to polish up his tarnished legacy, it would have to happen now. Having a patient clear out the clutter would keep his own hands clean."

"Bullshit," I said. "That's all bullshit."

"Probably," he said with a shrug. "But we need to know. We need to speak with patients. That's what I think."

"Yeah," I said with a colder chuckle than I had intended. "THAT'll sure be productive, all right."

"With your help, I'd like to meet with a few of Doctor Freeman's old charges. Just to see."

"To see what exactly? What do you hope they're going to tell us?"

"I don't know. That's what I want to find out. I've attempted to contact a number of Freeman's former patients on my own," he said, "and they are reticent to speak with me…those of them who are even capable of doing so."

I hated hearing that. I had deluded myself into thinking that the bulk of our former cases had gone on to lead moderately successful lives. Deep in the darker parts of my mind I suspected that it was a false notion, but I tried to convince myself all the same.

"I don't know what I'm doing wrong," Chris continued, "but there is something of a cultish air that continues to hang about Walter Freeman's reputation. His former patients appear very distrustful of doctors…except for The Man himself. And that makes me all the more suspicious. And it should do the same to you, quite frankly."

"He's got a certain thing about him," I said.

"But you're the inside man. They'll trust you, maybe. Or at least agree to a talk with you."

"So you want me to take a stab at it."

"I wouldn't have phrased it that way," he replied. "But yes. If you could."

"I'll see what I can do," I said. "I'll make a few phone calls. No promises, but what could it hurt."

We sat for a moment as the wind rustled in the leaves. Just beyond where his yard met the tree line I thought I saw movement in the brush. Looked almost like the shape of a person. But as soon as it came it was gone. I shrugged it off as a trick of the eyes, and a bit of buzz from the booze. Chris must have seen it too, however. He squinted his eyes as he peered out into the dark thatch of trees.

"Something?" he asked.

"Not sure," I answered. Whatever it was, it disappeared, and we didn't see it again.

"I've noticed," he said switching gears, "that a lot of your fellow orderlies at Riverside call you 'kid,' even though many of them are considerably younger than you are."

"Yeah, that actually came from a former patient of Walter's. Of *ours*. Doc Freeman always called me 'lad,' and the patient heard it, misremembered it as 'kid.' Like a dummy I mentioned it in conversation one time and it stuck. Lucky me."

"Who was the patient?"

The question took me out of myself for a moment. *Yes, who was the patient?* It had been so long since I had given it any thought that when the memory came back to me, it struck with a hard jolt.

"Salvador Reed," I said, more to myself than to Chris. "Yeah…yeah. Salvador Reed. Jesus Christ…You may have heard the name. He made the papers way back when. Before me and Doc got a hold of him."

"Sounds vaguely familiar."

"Raging psychotic. Good god-a-mighty. I've seen the batshit and the berserk in my time, believe me. But nothing like that guy. Tormented by violent hallucinations and paranoia. Said he could hear his dead relatives fucking and eating each other in Hell, and that government assassins had infiltrated the Vatican. Or maybe it was the other way around."

"It is interesting how many seriously disturbed patients I see who are Catholic. Or had been at one time."

"Well," I said, "with Salvador it was quite a bit more severe than being slapped around by a couple of warty old nuns. And his psychosis wasn't really the Church's fault…at least at first."

"The parents," he said. It wasn't a question.

"Isn't it always?"

"No. Not *always*."

"No doubt about it," I said, "that guy was destined to meet his end on death row for sure."

"Did he ever kill anyone?" Chris asked. I half-expected him to pull out a little spiral notebook and start jotting down some second-hand profile of Salvador Reed on the fly. It's actually rather surprising that he did not.

"It would only have been a matter of time," I answered. "Killed and mutilated several dogs, though. He did do that. Including a full-grown bull mastiff, which he ripped apart with his teeth and bare hands."

"It so often starts with animals," he said nodding, a bit of a twinkle in his eye.

"From the age of two his father had raped him and burned him with cigars," I continued. "Scorched him with boiling water, tossed him out a first-floor window when he was still in diapers."

"No mother?"

"Oh sure. He had a mother all right. And when he told her about what his father had done to him, she threw him down a flight of stairs. Both ma and pa were shot to death right in front of little Sal at age six by his mother's jealous lover. Story was, Salvador Reed had to be picked up and removed from their funeral because he started laughing. And he wouldn't stop. Just howling with laughter at the sight of their dead bodies. Imagine that, some little shaver at his folks' funeral just cackling like a mad thing."

"I can imagine it."

"He ended up in some Catholic orphanage where they beat him and locked him in his room for screaming out blasphemies in his sleep."

"You were raised in a Catholic orphanage too," Chris said, "were you not?"

"Yeah…" I answered, a bit put off by the question. "I was. What of it?"

"Just asking. Tell me more about Reed."

"He had to be isolated permanently as an adolescent for attempting to molest younger boys."

"Classic reflexive behavior for that type," Chris said. I sensed that he enjoyed the process of psychological profiling, regardless of the circumstances or content. I suppose that is why someone would go into this line of work after all.

I shuddered a bit, remembering Salvador Reed for the first time in over a decade. I suppose I had buried the memory under some old laundry in the back of my head. But there it was, there *he* was, and there was no shaking the image now. The wild, bloodshot eyes, the gnashing of gray, broken teeth, that hoarse bellowing…day and night…to only hear him from a distance you would have thought him a rabid animal instead of a human being.

"He surely was a monster, I'll tell ya that much," I said. "A made monster. Man alive was Walter proud of him."

"Proud of him?"

"Salvador was one of the first prefrontal lobotomies I ever assisted on. And he's what made me a true believer."

"Why is that?"

"First time I saw that guy I thought, Goddamn, somebody just kill this fucking beast and put it out of its misery. The only cure here's a shotgun blast to the face. I've never quaked in my boots harder, and that's no jive. 'You sure these leather restraints are gonna hold him?' I kept asking. 'We're sure about that, right, Doc?' Walter just smiled. Never nervous. Always confident. He loved the challenge."

"Sure."

"So we shocked him under, Walter began the old pop n' scramble, and a half an hour later, Salvador Reed awoke…a brand-new man. Just as calm, kind, and soft-spoken a gentleman as you'd ever like to meet."

"Any cognitive awareness?"

"Completely. Deeply remorseful of past offenses, fully self-aware, determined to start over fresh. He was truly and completely…*healed*."

"You're sure about that?"

"As I live and breathe…to the extent that I do either." I chuckled a bit at the memory. "First thing he said when he came to," I said, "you're gonna love this…very first words out of his mouth…*I forgive them*."

"*I forgive them*," Chris repeated. He did not chuckle along with me. I could tell he was mentally jotting down notes.

"If I'm lying I'm dying," I said. "*I forgive them*. He forgave his parents. First words. He forgave them for what they had done to him. I was flabbergasted. I think even Walter was surprised by the success, although he never let on. I know he would have loved to drag old Sal out on the road with us as a living model for the wonders of the transorbital lobotomy, like he had done to some of the others. But it wasn't to be."

"Whatever happened to him?"

"Reed's older, previously estranged half-sister appeared from out of nowhere and swept him off to a quiet little hideaway in Ashburn, Virginia. And that's the long and the short of it. I'd never seen such a strong case for the lobotomy…Haven't seen one since either."

"So no ill effects whatever?"

"He could never read or write again, but that was it as far as I know."

"Ashburn, you say?" Chris said, tapping his pointed chin with his index finger. "What's that, an eight-hour drive from here?"

"Give or take."

"I'd love to meet him."

"He won't talk to you, Doc," I said, polishing off my drink. "Trust me. I doubt he'd talk to *me*, even though I tried to keep up with him for a while. Don't get me wrong, he'd be friendly and courteous, and maybe whittle you something out of an old log. But that'd be the end of the line. Salvador Reed doesn't make new friends. He doesn't even own a telephone."

I pondered for a moment the idea of old Sal as a suspect. It seemed impossible on so many fronts. In his wild, pre-lobotomy state he was hardly one to sneak around and cover up his violence. And the man he was as I saw him last...just didn't seem the type.

"It's like I'm saying, Chris," I said, "I'll make the calls and see who'll chat with us. But I don't know that there's anything to find out there."

"We have to try," he said, compulsively crunching his ice cubes. "Another doctor turns up dead and...I don't know...I will feel personally responsible."

"There's only so much we can do. You know that as well as I do."

"And how would you feel," he said, "if that next victim is Dr. Freeman himself?"

"I...yeah." A horrible chill shot through me. I couldn't stand the thought of anyone hurting Dr. Freeman, even as I considered everyone he had hurt. "We'll do what we can. If there is something out there, we'll find it."

"Or it'll find us," he said.

"Yeah. Or that."

I stared out into the brush again, eyes peeled for whatever may be out there.

Nothing. It's nothing.

CHAPTER 15

Driving down Route 65 toward the Western Pennsylvania Hospital for the Insane, I was nearly blown out of my seat for the déjà vu. Time was, this had been a real swanky establishment. Just outside of Pittsburgh, it had all the amenities: Lush, green gardens, croquet courts, a baseball diamond, *the works*. Seeing old pictures of the grounds, you would have thought it more a country club than a bughouse.

By the time *I* ended up working the floors there, however, there was no mistaking that it was a just trash dump for the shunned and the unwanted. Patients wandered the halls unattended, moaning, screaming, soiling themselves, banging their heads against the walls. You wouldn't believe the smell. I was shocked by the conditions at first, and did what I could to help. But it wasn't much. Occasionally I got the feeling that I was the only one working there who cared at all.

And then, thankfully, I stopped caring.

The hopelessness of it all was oddly liberating. I used to get drunk down in the old in-house morgue, and no one ever noticed. I likely could have stopped showing up for work and still collected a paycheck without much attention on me for a quite a good while.

In fact, that is precisely what I did.

When Chris and I arrived I was pleased to see that they were trying to make improvements, but there is only so much that can be done at the end of the day. I predicted they would be shutting the doors before long. Chris concurred.

"It's a good thing we made it here before that happens," he said.

They practically shut the doors *on us*, to tell the honest truth. It was made clear that we were not welcome (or, rather, *I* wasn't), and we were more or less shown the exit the moment we set foot on the weedy, unkempt grounds. No matter. The last of Doc Freeman's patients who had been permanent residents there had died by then anyway, so the trip was nearly a whole lotta nothing for nothing.

However, we managed to get our hands on a couple of old records that gave us the names of three women all living together in a communal row house in Wheeling, West Virginia. Two sisters and a second cousin. All former patients of Dr. Walter Freeman. All moderately well-functioning. And so, away we went.

Traveling with Dr. Chris Williams definitely had its perks. Nice hotels, sizable suites, it was a different side of life from what I was accustomed, no doubt about that. Back in the Freeman days it was taken as a given that Walter and I would do our own separate things when we weren't working, and I think we both liked it that way just fine.

But, either Chris just really enjoyed my company, or he simply felt no compunction to take in the local color out on the road. We were always together, and nearly always discussing *the task at hand*. And nothing but. Just as well. But for shoptalk, I doubt he and I would have had much in common anyhow.

Different from Doc Freeman as well, Chris *hated* traveling. For the short bursts we were out, I could tell he wanted to get back to Poughkeepsie as soon as possible. Not a problem. Different strokes and all of that. We had planned it out that, when he needed to take the train back to New York so as not to fall too far behind in his duties, I would continue on without him, expenses paid. (How he convinced Riverside to allow me to do this I never found out. And, of course, I couldn't give less of a shit.) We would then

reconvene, powwow on progress (if any), and repeat.
Fancy digs and an open bar tab…hell. A fella could get used to this detective business.

"Would you fellows like to join us for brunch?"
"Yes, could you stay?"
"Could you?"
Harriet, Marie and Dorothy Kayland were their names, but I could not get a handle on which was who and whatnot. You would have taken them for triplets if you didn't know better, and no fooling.
The Kayland Gals shared a tidy little nest in suburban Wheeling, paid for by a modest but significant trust fund. As far as I could tell, they spent their days tending to their vast array of white orchids and shopping for matching powder-blue bonnets. If I were to wager on their ages, I would say somewhere in the mid-to-late 50s. But truthfully, I could not gauge it. Their pure white smiles and only vaguely vacant expressions indicated nothing in the way of life experience. Such is the wonder of *the procedure,* after all. It wipes the boards clean.
The ladies must have been patients after my time (or possibly before), as I had no memory of them. However, they were positive that they had met me before.
"Oh yes, most definitely, you were with Doctor Freeman!"
"Yes, you were with him for sure!"
"For sure."
"Could you tell us," Chris asked them as we munched on ladyfingers and sipped Darjeeling, "about the last time you saw Doctor Freeman?"
"Oh, Walter Freeman is such a lovely man."
"Yes, he really is just lovely."
"Just lovely."
It seemed clear to me early on in the visit that we were not going to get far, and began trying to concoct a polite exit strategy.

All the while Chris asked them about medications they may be taking (aspirin and calcium supplements), any difficulties they may have experienced since their respective surgeries (*None* they said, although I'd beg to differ), and if they've ever seen another doctor besides Walter Freeman.

"Oh, there have been a few other doctors."

"Yes, a few of them have stopped by."

"Just a few."

They could not seem to name any, however two of them were sure that one young physician come a-calling, in fact, was *yours truly*.

"Wasn't that you, good sir?"

"You're the young doctor who came some years ago, yes?"

"Ma'ams," I said, "I assure you, I've never been here before. And I'm not a doctor, I'm simply a—"

"No no," said the voice of dissent, "that young doctor was taller than he is. Yes. The one with the hair? He was taller. And darker. Much darker."

"What do you mean *darker*?" Chris asked.

"Darker like you, Doctor," she replied to Chris.

I looked over at Chris's fair hair and pale skin and wondered what the fuck we thought we were doing there.

"Don't mind her," her sister and/or cousin said, "she confuses easily."

"Yes, on occasion, she confuses dreams for real life."

"Yes, don't mind me."

We thanked the Ladies Kayland for their time and hospitality and made our exit. They extended an open invitation to visit any time and to give our regards to Dr. Freeman. We said we surely would. I heard a bottle calling out to me. And an ampoule as well.

That night we stayed at the McClure Hotel in lovely downtown Wheeling, and I thought it really was something special. Chris said he thought it was "just fine," but it was the fanciest joint I had ever stayed in, I can tell you that much.

For dinner we had steaks, scalloped potatoes and Cognac. I was informed that brandy is meant to be drunk *after* dinner, but why wait, I say. Chris shrugged and drank his with the meal as well.

"You know what I have not seen in Wheeling, West Virginia?" I said, somewhat rhetorically. "The rock n' roll kids."

"Beg pardon?"

"You know, the cats with long hair, the girls with no shoes on, the beads and ripped dungarees. You know. Rock n' roll. I mean, there are a few. But not many at all. Not that I've seen."

"I saw one earlier today," he said. "Across the street in fact. When we were coming to check in. Big fellow. Black rain jacket. You could barely see his face for the hair and the beard."

"Really? I didn't notice him."

"You were already inside. I waved, but he just shuffled away. They take a lot of drugs, those kids. It's a sad thing."

"Yeah," I replied, feeling more than a bit hypocritical. "I've heard that." I shoveled a forkful of potatoes into my mouth and hoped the subject would change.

"I thought West Virginia would be the mother lode for our purposes," Chris said. "I thought we'd have our pick of patients with whom to speak."

"Because of Operation Ice Pick?" I said. "I thought so too."

"Nearly three hundred transorbital lobotomies in…what was it, two weeks?"

"Something like that. Two hundred and eighty-eight, if I remember correctly."

"Where did they all go," he asked the air all around. "Where did they go?"

All of those state-sponsored operations through West Virginia, and the only patients we could find were the Kayland Gals. And we only discovered them by accident.

"You think those three women we saw today were part of that Operation Ice Pick thing?" Chris asked. "That would explain why they thought they recognized you but you don't remember them. You may have been their last memory pre-lobotomy, but they'd just be three faces in a big crowd to you."

"It's entirely possible," I said. "I have almost no tangible memory of that time at all. I split from Doc Freeman not too long after that. Course I don't have much tangible memory of that either."

"Were you just drunk?" he asked. "Or were you high?"

That was the first time he ever openly mentioned my habit. I never got the sense that he disapproved, but I was sure that the curiosity regarding its effects would get the best of him eventually.

"Now Chris," I said, "you should know better. You're a doctor after all. Thorazine doesn't get you high."

"I only know what I've read," he said. "I've never bought the line that it was in any way comparable to an actual prefrontal lobotomy."

"Couldn't tell ya, man," I said. "I don't have enough to go on. But I can say that it does make life slightly less of an excruciating ordeal."

"It seemed like one shouldn't drink alcohol in tandem with it, though."

"One probably shouldn't drink alcohol in tandem with *anything*, Doc. But here we are."

"*Touché.*"

We clinked glasses.

"Here's the thing on the two-eighty-eight," I said, "because of the assembly-line nature of that whole scene, there wasn't much in the way of paperwork I think. They weren't our regulars. If there are records, I sure don't know where they are."

"Perhaps Freeman does."

"Maybe. But I doubt it. I'll bet I can find out more, but I'll need some time. We may have to double back down this way. In the meanwhile, we're hitting Louisville, Kentucky tomorrow. Bout a five-hour drive."

"Oh joy."

"Indeed."

"Would you gentlemen care for any dessert?" the waiter asked. I hadn't noticed him approach the table.

"Just a bit more Cognac," Chris said, "yeah?"

"You know I'm game," I said. The waiter nodded and went off to fetch a fresh bottle.

"Word of warning," Chris said, "Brandy is pretty much a guaranteed hangover."

"Oh well," I said, scraping the last bit of meat that I could from my T-bone. "I tend not to worry too much about how I'm going to feel the next day. It's a general philosophy I live by."

Chris laughed heartily. He tended toward the dour side, and this was the first true laugh I had ever heard come out of him.

"What a philosophy," he said.

"It's what has made me the success I am today."

We shot the shit for a little while longer, then headed on up to our respective rooms. Because they had no double suites available, Chris went ahead and got me my own room for the night. I flipped on the television briefly, but there was nothing but the war on every channel. I'd also ended up with the bottle of Cognac, and proceeded to take it to bed with me. Despite the dire warning, it was the best night's sleep I'd had since as long as I could remember...

...Until I found myself awakened by a broom handle jabbing repeatedly into my ribcage.

"Hey hey hey!" I said, dizzy and disoriented, my eyes a blur. "What's the gag?"

The jabbing ceased, and I sat up straight. The mist cleared, and I saw Chris standing near my bed, but a good distance off, brandishing a broom like a jouster's lance. Next to him stood an elderly, dark-skinned woman in a maid's uniform, her head cocked cryptically to the side.

"It's time to get up," Chris said, more than slightly perturbed. "We're late. We should have gotten on the road two hours ago. I tried calling your room several times and you didn't answer. The hotel was about to call an ambulance. Thankfully this fine woman here opened the door for me with her master key."

"All right, all right," I said with a stretch, "and poking me in the ribs with a long stick was called for?"

"I thought it safer for all concerned," he said.

I looked down at myself and realized that I was still fully dressed, boots and all, and laying atop a still-made bed. The bottle lay empty on its side next to me. And clutched in my right hand was my buck knife, sharp and fully extended.

"Um yes…" I said, more than a bit embarrassed. I flipped the blade closed, returned it to its holster on my belt, and stood up to brush out the wrinkles from my clothes. "Always good to be prepared for any contingency, that's my motto. It's kind of a scout thing, you understand. Always prepared."

"Absolutely," Chris said, not lowering the stick, "I couldn't agree more."

CHAPTER 16

"Hello?" I said, knocking on the cracked oak door. "Mrs. O'Dell?"

In the twenty years that had passed since the last time I had set foot on this porch, not a tremendous amount appeared to have changed. The livestock were gone, and there appeared to be new construction across the duck pond, but that was a ways off.

"I'm a-comin'," we heard a voice say from within. "I'm a-comin'."

"Nice place," Chris said, rocking back on his heels. I couldn't tell if he was being sarcastic or not.

Of the people I had called on the telephone to meet with us, Gertrude O'Dell was far and away the most enthusiastic. Without needing much of anything in the way of details she invited us out to their Louisville, Kentucky farmhouse for a chat. It was heartening to speak with someone so unambiguously pleased with the results of her husband's procedure. I doubted Eugene O'Dell would have much to offer in the way of clues or information, but part of me really just wanted to show off a success to Dr. Williams.

The door opened with a creak, and Gertrude O'Dell appeared on the other side, smiling warmly in what I would assume was her Sunday best. A plain and pleasant woman of a certain age, clearly she had fixed herself up for company.

"Hello, Mrs. O'Dell. You remember me, ma'am?" I asked.

"Well, of course, darlin'," she laughed, throwing her arms

around me in an embrace I surely didn't deserve. "It's so good to see you again after all this time!"

"Twenty years, nearly."

"My heavens, where does the time go."

"This is my friend, Dr. Chris Williams."

"Welcome, Dr. Williams, welcome," she said, shaking Chris's hand. "Welcome to the O'Dell estate." She laughed a bit at her own joke, and we did as well.

"Thank you, ma'am."

"Come in, please!"

We did. The décor was just as I had remembered, but blessedly gone were the piglets and chickens. In their stead was a well-worn softness. The house smelled of cinnamon apples.

"We really appreciate you meeting with us, Mrs. O'Dell," Chris said.

"Nothing of it. My pleasure. Have a sit," she replied. "Can I git y'all a soda? Or ice water? Or pie?"

"Ice water would be lovely, ma'am," Chris said.

"Comin' right up!" and she scurried off as we took our places on the flowered sofa.

"Twenty years," I whispered to Chris. "Jesus. Last time I was here they didn't even have a refrigerator." No sooner did the words leave my mouth, when the sound of a block of ice being broken with an ice pick was heard. Some things, indeed, never change.

"So Mrs. O'Dell," I shouted toward the kitchen, "how have you been?"

"Couldn't be better, darlin'!" she chirped in reply.

"And Mr. O'Dell?"

"Good as gold and sweeter'n honey! I'll fetch him in a jiffer."

She entered with two glasses of ice water and a plate of Nutter Butter cookies. I hopped up to help her with the plate.

"Thank you, ma'am," said Chris, taking his drink.

"I do have to warn y'all," she said as she sat down on the opposing divan, "Eugene ain't a big one fer chattin' these days…but then, he never was at that."

"We understand," I said. "So over the years, there have never been any adverse reactions to the procedure? Nothing at all? We've heard of occasional short-term memory loss. Some difficulty with numbers. Nothing of that sort?"

"We got no complaints, hon. Not a one in the world."

"Has Dr. Freeman been by to see you folks recently?" I asked.

"Well he surely has, and plenty too. I been a-wonderin' where you done gone to, sweetheart. I thought you and ol' Doc Freeman was like two peas."

"Well, you know how it is, ma'am," I said. "Sometimes people just go their separate ways." She smiled sweetly, but clearly had no comprehension of people going their separate ways. "So," I went on, "were these visits business or pleasure?"

"Oh, you know Doc Freeman. There really ain't no separatin' the two."

"Ain't it the truth."

We laughed and clinked our glasses.

"Could we speak with your husband, Mrs. O'Dell?" Chris asked, eager to move this thing along.

"Reckon he's right in the other room," she said.

She turned her head to the side and said in a slightly higher voice, as if she were calling to a small child, "Gene-y? Some folks is here to visit with you, sweetie." Nothing. She shrugged, sighed lightly, and said to us, "Be right back."

She walked into the other room. A moment later she returned, guiding the large man very slowly by the hand. Eugene shuffled awkwardly, a bland grin across his otherwise blank face. His eyes were barely open and his head shook ever so slightly. *Holy Christ in heaven…*Not knowing what else to do, I stood to help, but Gertrude waved me off. I felt as though I may get sick.

"Hell…Hello, Mr. O'Dell," I said trying to mask my horror. "It's…great to see you again…after all this time."

"Huuuunnnnnn…" Eugene replied, humming like a small electric generator. "The thingssssss…"

"Mr. O'Dell," Chris said, cool and professional, although I

could tell he was taken aback as well, "My name is Dr. Williams. I would really like to speak with you, if you don't mind."

"Ynnnnngggsssss…"

"How are you feeling today, sir?"

"Huuunnnnn…the thingsssss…Like that…thingssss…"

"Git used to that," Gertrude chuckled, "You gonna hear a mess of it." She helped him sit on the couch. "You want a glass of water, honey-pie?"

He murmured and shook his head *No* like an enormous toddler. She sat next to him, continuing to hold his hand lovingly. I struggled to hold back my nausea.

You did this to him…you did this…you did this…

"Mr. O'Dell," Chris asked, "Eugene, do you recall meeting with Dr. Freeman recently?"

"Hnnnnnnnn…" Eugene replied, nodding slightly, "Things…hnnnn…"

"And was he happy with your progress?"

Eugene continued to nod. "Thingsss…good things…like that…hnnnn…"

"And…" I interjected, although perhaps I should not have, "how…how are *you*? Sir? Are you…are you happy, Mr. O'Dell?" I couldn't help myself.

"We couldn't be happier, could we Gene-y?" Gertrude piped in, squeezing Eugene's large bicep. Eugene's head proceeded to both nod and shake.

"Hnnnnnn…things…"

"Good things!" Gertrude chirped.

"Hnnnn…Love…you…Trudie…"

"Oh," she beamed, kissing him on the cheek, "you silly ol' bear."

I was astonished at how pleased she seemed. How could she possibly be so happy being married to someone who was, in effect, a large, mindless infant? I couldn't restrain myself any longer.

"Mrs. O'Dell," I said, "Ma'am…"

"Yes, dear?"

"I feel like I…Oh God. I owe you…I mean to say…there are

no words to express how…sorry…I mean…"

"Sorry, dear?" she said, furrowing her brow ever so slightly. "What for?"

"You've been left as a…as a full-time caregiver. And this was…NEVER…Never was my…never was our intention…to…" My voice shook. My hands shook. I needed a drink and a needle and I needed to run. Chris and Mrs. O'Dell stared at me, and I knew I should have kept my mouth shut. But I couldn't. "I'm sorry, ma'am." This was why. This was why I had to get away from Dr. Freeman. Because he…because we…created idiot children like Eugene O'Dell. "I'm…just…" This was our medicine. This is what we had done. "I'm so sorry."

And the room fell still.

Gertrude released Eugene's hand. He continued to sit, grinning blankly, his head shaking slightly. She, however, was suddenly more serious than she had been. Not angry or severe…but more serious. She eyed me closely for a moment. Suddenly, in a high voice she said,

"Ooooo, thunder, Gene-y!"

Eugene shut his eyes tightly and covered his ears.

Silence.

When she spoke again, it was very matter-of-fact, a side of her we had not yet seen. "Let me ask y'all somethin'," she said, leaning in toward us. "You ever find yerself needin' to sleep with one eye open and a sharp knife under yer pillow?"

"Yes ma'am," I said without hesitation. "Quite often."

"No ma'am," said Chris. "I cannot say that I have."

"Do you know what it's like to never know who yer gonna wake up next to in the mornin'?"

Well…yes, I thought, but kept quiet. So did Chris.

"Do you know what it's like to go to sleep at night in the arms of the sweetest fella you ever met, and wake up next to a ravin', slobberin' animal who'll beat you with a curtain rod because a talkin' smoke bush told him to? Do you know what it's like to live in constant fear that yer high school sweetheart, the love of yer life, might just up and cut out yer heart one day? Just because? On account of tiny angels what live in his ear? Do you know what it's like to wonder if you got it in you to kill someone you love fer to keep yer own self alive? Do you?"

She paused for a moment as we all considered the situation.

Finally she said, "Now, am I right in thinkin' that y'all are NOT comin' round here tryin' to dig up dirt on Doctor Walter Freeman? 'Cause I'm sure that ain't what this is all about."

We'd run into this sort thing before, although usually just on the telephone. Folks were either suspicious of you because they hated Walter Freeman, and you by extension...or they were lightning quick to take up for him if they suspected that you're even slightly on the wrong side of righteousness.

"That's absolutely not what's going on, ma'am," I answered. "You know as well as anyone that Doc Freeman is my very dear friend. Two peas, right?"

"Doctor Freeman is my hero, ma'am," Chris said. "He is the reason I became the doctor that I am today. I attended one of his lectures eighteen years ago, and from then on my path in life was set."

"That's good," she said with a smile and a nod. "That's real good to hear."

She gently lifted Eugene's left hand from his ear, and in a motherly tone said,

"Thunder's all gone, Gene-y. It's safe now."

Eugene opened his eyes and uncovered his ears.

"You see," Gertrude continued, "Doc Freeman ain't just saved my husband. He saved me. He saved my life, and he gave me a life. There is a special spot in heaven set aside just for Walter Freeman, and I reckon it still won't be worthy of him. He's an angel here on earth, and I'd cuss and spit on anyone who'd dare speak ill of—or wish ill will upon—that man."

"We understand," Chris said. "And truth be told, ma'am, although I can't say too much about it, that's just precisely why we came calling today. I will say that we're just hoping to keep our fellow doctors—Doctor Freeman most of all—and all of their patients, safe and sound. That's our only goal."

"Well that's the Lord's work yer doin' then, darlin'. God bless you for it."

She took my empty water glass off to the kitchen, leaving us alone with Eugene. He simply sat, vibrating blankly.

After a long, excruciating pause I said,

"Um...I'm glad you are doing well, Mr. O'Dell."

"Hmmmmm..." he replied. "Hnnnnnn...he things...the thingsss..."

"Yes," I said. "The things."

"The thingsssss...hhhnnnnnn..."

"You said it, sir. You said it."

"The things...will kill...will kill...hnnnnn..."

Chris choked on the last of his water. "How's that, sir?"

Eugene continued to smile blandly.

"Kill...hmmm...will kill...the things kill..."

"Kill?" Chris asked. "Who is going to kill, Eugene?"

"Hmm-hunnnnn...the things..."

"Please, Mr. O'Dell," I said urgently, "what do you mean by 'will kill'? Who is? What is?"

Eugene's vacant eyes suddenly shot open completely, two empty globes of cold marble, and stared directly at Chris—

"Thingsss...kill...doc...hollow...kill..." He tried to snap his fingers, "like that..."

"What? What does that mean?" I pressed further, feeling myself look at Chris askance out of the corner of my eye. "Which Doc? This Doc? Dr. Chris Williams here?"

"Do you mean Doc Freeman?" Chris asked him. "Do you feel hollow, Mr. O'Dell? Is that what you're saying?"

"Doc...holloowwwww..." Eugene said, still directly at Chris, his tone of voice warbled, like a vinyl record warped by the sun. "Hollowwww...ynnnnggzzzz doc...hollowwww..."

"Mrs. O'Dell," Chris shouted to the kitchen, "can you make sense of this 'hollow' business?"

Gertrude entered casually.

"Just one of Gene-y's new noises," she said with a shrug. "Started addin' it to his repertoire of gibberish after the last time Dr. Freeman came to call. Nothin' to git in a twist over, I don't reckon."

Eugene shook his head harder, and leaned in close to Chris and me. Hissing, nearly growling,

"Doc...holloooooowwww..."

Gertrude came back over and took her seat next to her husband. Eugene soon calmed again, and it was as if nothing had happened.

"Well...thank...uh...thank you both so much for your time," Chris said, standing. I followed suit. "We should really be heading on back to Poughkeepsie."

"Aw, so soon?" Gertrude said.

"Sadly yes," Chris replied. "Business to attend to and all of that. And it's a bit of a haul back to New York."

"Well, you be sure to give ol' Doc Freeman our love now," Gertrude said as we moved to the door. "And feel free to stop on by any ol' time. We're always here!"

"Surely will, ma'am," I said. "Thanks again." I turned to Eugene and said, "Take care now, Mr. O'Dell."

"Ynnnngggzzzz...hnnnn...thingssss..."

CHAPTER 17

Chris accompanied me to visit two more former patients before heading back to Riverside:

Lucy Moore, nearly catatonic, like a statue in her parents' front parlor. Said just about nothing to us. *Just about.* Ronald Berkley, conversely, was very talkative indeed, although I could hardly understand him for all the hooting and whooping. His brother and his brother's wife, who had taken on the responsibility of looking after him, were polite enough to us. But they remembered me. And if their eyes had been shotguns, there'd be not much left of me, believe that.

Both Lucy and Ronald, however, different though their states may have been, had something very similar to say upon seeing us (or Chris, specifically). A two words to whisper and hiss…

Doc…hollow…

No specifics. No context. Just the noise.

Doc…hollllllowwww…

Chris was exactly correct about what the police reaction would be. We contacted three separate departments to explain to them who we were and what we had discovered in our travels.

"We'll file a report, sirs," is all we got in return.

"We already filed a report!"

"We'll add to the existing report, then."

I can't say that I blamed them, though. It was nearly impossible to explain the crimes that we felt had been committed. "Dead lobotomists! The cryptic, albeit identical, jabbering of nearly brain-dead mental patients! Don't you see the connection!?!?"

We sounded as screwy as the patients we were neglecting back in Poughkeepsie.

As we drove through Ohio on our way to Union Station Chris seemed particularly agitated. I could not tell if he thought the trip yielded fruit, and he was not forthcoming with conversation in general. We bade farewell at the train station, and I headed on my way. It was a long drive, and I found myself oddly eager to get back to Washington DC. But I decided, before heading on into DC proper, that I should try to make a stop in Ashburn.

CHAPTER 18

Minor difficulties notwithstanding, Salvador Reed managed to get by just swell carving and selling homemade duck decoys to local hunters. A far cry from the man who once tried, and very nearly succeeded, to murder two Catholic priests simultaneously with a single line of piano wire.

Salvador's cottage was nestled in a sleepy little pocket of farmland, a near-perfect physical manifestation of the man's demeanor.

"More tea?" Salvador asked me, the very picture of serenity.

I have to say, I was a bit surprised that he remembered me. I had always seen my role in the procedure as being relatively minor. But patients did often seem to relate to me in a way that they likely could not have with Doctor Freeman. Doctors can be intimidating, after all. They have power over the rest of us. But me? I'm just a regular cat, don't you know.

"Thank you, Mr. Reed. It's really great to see you. And to find you doing so well. It's a definite relief after what I've seen recently."

"Well," he replied in a voice so soft I nearly had to strain to hear him, "we're all different. Yes? What's good for one is not so good for all. For me? No regrets. I remember the ogre that I was once, and I don't ever want to be that again."

Baxter, Salvador's old bloodhound, rested his floppy jowls on my knee. I patted his head and thought, *If only you knew what your master used to do to furry old fellas like you.*

"So no problems at all?" I asked.

"Well…"

"Yes, the reading and writing, of course."

"Thankfully my sister has been a dear about helping me with the technical side of my business. Her health has been failing her recently, the poor thing. But we look after each other well. Her children were frightened of me for a long time. And who could blame them. But they know I'm different now. Now I'm just old uncle Sal."

He chuckled lightly, blew on his tea, then did not take a sip.

"Your ducks are really beautiful," I said admiring the handiwork that lined the walls of his modest cabin. "It's like they have separate personalities."

"Yes," he said, endlessly stirring his well-sugared cup. "It's almost a shame to put them in the water. But it is their purpose. Purpose is good. It's a real good thing. Purpose. It's good. To have a purpose. More tea?"

"I have a full cup, thank you. Mr. Reed?"

"Yes?"

"You used to suffer hallucinations."

"Oh, I did indeed. Yes. Ugly things. Demons coming out of the walls." He shuddered. "They would scream all night that I would burn forever in Hell if I didn't obey them. Awful business."

"I'm sorry to bring it back up."

"No, it's OK. It's good to talk through it. It's good. More tea?"

"No, thank you. So you've had no flashbacks?"

"None that I can think of. Can I get you some more tea?"

"Um…"

"There is one," he said, still very soft and calm. "It's more of a nightmare, really. Not so much a hallucination than a bad dream. Would you like some tea? I thought I'd make a pot."

"Well, uh, we have tea already, sir."

"Oh," he chuckled lightly in surprise, "so we do." He shrugged and sipped happily.

"Can you tell me about this nightmare?"

"Oh, it's silly, really. I only mention it because you asked." He paused, then said, "It has happened a couple of times. A repeating dream. But it shouldn't concern you. It doesn't concern me. Outside Baxter?"

The old hound looked at him, tail wagging, but continued to rest his chin on my leg.

"Please, sir, if you don't mind. I'm curious."

"Well…OK, if I must." He sat, looking contemplative for a moment. When he spoke again, it was still soft and calm, but distant. "A dark figure comes to me in the night. I can't see its face, but it knows my name."

"Is it a man or a woman?"

"I can't tell, but it's pretty big. I don't think it's either a man or a woman, really. Just a shape. A hood. A tangle of hair. Just a phantom. It growls in a monotone all of these ugly things about revenge and violence, all of the terrible things that used to possess me so many years ago. I tell it to go away, and it insists that I will join it someday."

"Was it like the demons you used to see? The ones that told you to harm people?"

"No. Not like those."

"No?"

"It's different from them."

"How so?"

"It's different."

"Different in what way?"

"It's a person."

"I see. Does it tell you its name?"

"No, it doesn't seem to have one. It just says that I…*will kill*. Or rather *we will kill*."

Oh fuck…I thought.

"Go on please," I said.

"It is quite dreadful, kid, I must say. That's still your nickname? Dr. Freeman always called you 'kid.' But it's just a bad dream. Like lingering residue from the old Sal. But thankfully, he's mostly dead now. Mostly. More tea?"

"Mr. Reed...are you sure it's just a dream?"

"What do you mean? More tea?"

"Yes, thank you. I'd love some. I mean...does it feel *real* to you?"

"Well...it does, yes. I mean to say, as real as anything seems to me now."

"Oh?"

"One clear change from the operation...I now always feel as if I'm caught halfway between sleep and waking. Never fully one or the other. But as I said, it's much preferred over the old Salvador. I think I'll make a pot of tea, would you like some?"

"No thank you. Mr. Reed...has this nightmare figure ever told you its name?" I've found that sometimes lobotomy patients need to have the same question asked in different ways for them to connect with it.

"Oh, no. I don't think I've given it a name."

"I see."

"It does claim to be a doctor, though."

Oh...Of course it does...

"Just a nameless doctor?"

"No name. But it tells me how it feels. And it insists that I feel the same as it does. More tea?"

"And...how does it feel?"

"Hollow. It's hollow."

Goddamn it all...

"And...do you feel that way, Mr. Reed? Do you share the dark figure's feeling? Do you feel hollow?"

"Well, yes," he said with a slight nod. "A bit. But I would rather feel hollow than filled up with rage. More tea?"

"I should be getting back to work. It's been good to see you, Mr. Reed."

"I'm sure we'll see each other again very soon," he said.

"I certainly hope we do."

"I am sure of it. Very soon. *I am sure of it.*"

***

Lucy Moore, Salvador Reed, Ronald Berkley, Eugene O'Dell…all former patients, with varying degrees of damage, all from different sections of the country, all with an odd noise buried within their respective jumbles of murmuring, mumbling, clicking and ticking—

Doc…Hollow…

Had they met? How could they have?

Doc…Hollow…

I thought I knew what it meant, but I wasn't really sure. It seemed like a name at first. But then I thought that it might be a statement. As in "The Doc is hollow." Or "Doc, I am hollow." Or… "Doc has left me hollow."

Truthfully, I didn't know a goddamn thing. I was no sleuth; that was clear. I was drained. Empty. I had hit a wall. And with not much of anything to go on, I was heading on back to DC.

CHAPTER 19

"All right there, Walter?"

"Ah," Freeman said rising to stand at his desk, offering me the glad hand. "Here you are, lad. Good to see you. I trust you've been well."

Although he was pleasant enough, as always, Dr. Freeman appeared otherwise non-nonplussed to see me.

"I'm eating," I said. "Thirteen years, Doc. Can you believe it?"

"Has it really been that long? I hadn't noticed I suppose."

"How is everyone? Marjorie and the girls?"

He smiled, but didn't answer. He came around from the desk and indicated the tanned leather couch. *What the hell, do all these brain doctors order their furniture from the same fucking catalogue?!*

"Please, have a seat," he said. We both did. It was good to see him. And it was more awkward than I thought it would be.

"So how is Riverside holding up?" he asked, with what seemed to be genuine interest.

"Not too well," I said truthfully. "A bit on the decline to be perfectly honest."

"Well, who is surprised by that?" he huffed. "Sometimes I wonder why these people even bother holding symposia."

Here we go, I thought.

"Ideas," he said, "solid ideas, are bandied about, serious

discussions are *hurrumphed* over. And then, ultimately, everyone just sticks with the old routines. Roger Cook never listens to me."

"Everyone listens to you, Walter," I said, "for some reason."

That was a bit more perfectly honest than I had really intended.

"Oh?"

"Not that they shouldn't," I said, trying to recover. "Sorry. That came out wrong."

"Hm, yes," he said, nodding stiffly. "Yes indeed. So to what do I owe this pleasure today? What's on your mind?"

"Dead lobotomists. Not to put too fine a point on it. Seventeen of them."

"Ah. Well, that's cheery."

"It's all the talk 'round the soda shop these days."

"I hadn't heard seventeen. Depends upon when you start counting, I suppose." He gave a little cryptic chuckle, then said, "Grim business at Longview Asylum in Cincinnati, Ohio this past week. You heard about that, yes?"

"I had not."

"I haven't heard much in the way of details."

"Someone died at Longview?"

"Did you ever work those floors?"

"Briefly. Who was it?"

"No one with whom I was familiar," he said. "Some *psycho-analyst*." The contempt in his voice was tangible.

"Name?"

"I suppose, but none known to me."

"I wonder," I said, "if the victim had ever attended one your lectures…"

"What a queer thing to say," he replied. "What could possibly be the relevance of that?"

"I don't know. Just talking is all."

"And you're presuming foul play. I'd say 'casualty' instead of 'victim,' until the facts are in."

"So what killed this nameless doctor?"

"Drug overdose, apparently," Walter said, clucking his tongue for the shame of it all. "They found the needle still stuck in his cold, swollen arm. When will people learn..."

"Heh. Yeah."

"Eerily enough," he continued, "I happened to be passing through Southern Ohio around that same time. It's a funny thing." I nearly told him that we had been passing through those parts about that time as well, but thought better of it.

"Enough of this morbid talk," he said. "Tell me all about yourself these days."

"You're looking at it."

"Oh, come now."

"I'm concerned for your safety, Walter."

"I appreciate your concern, lad," he sighed, "but let's not make much ado about little, all right?"

"I didn't think it was anything either at first," I said, "I laughed it off. But now...I'm not so sure."

"People die," he said casually, removing his perpetually scratched, perfect-circle spectacles. He cleaned them on his shirt and then dropped them into his vest pocket. "That's how the cookie crumbles. Yes? There is nothing more to it than the random nature of life itself. Trust me, my boy, no one was the least bit concerned until Bruce Haines passed on."

"He was killed," I said. "He was *murdered*."

"Sad business that, to be sure. But everything was just hunky-dory until Haines died. Then, all of the sudden, we're hearing rubbish about 'patterns,' and 'red flags' and 'the general ignorance of law enforcement these days.' And now we've got some Chris Williams character crawling out of the cupboards thinking he's Basil Rathbone."

"Basil Rathbone died just recently."

"Oh?" Freeman chuckled, squinting, as if he didn't *want* to see me clearly. "Was he a lobotomist too?"

"So you've spoken with Chris?"

"You know this crackpot?" Freeman asked. He squinted at me sideways, but did not retrieve his glasses. "Oh yes, I suppose you would." He waved his hand dismissively. "He is at Riverside, isn't he? My dear boy, listen. I put up with enough delusion and balderdash from my patients. I'd rather not get it from my colleagues. You tell Dr. Williams to tend to his charges and focus his concern on them. I'm sure that's more than enough to keep him occupied."

"I'll pass that along."

"Much appreciated."

"So you don't find anything peculiar about the situation?"

"I find *everything* peculiar, lad. Everything."

The conversation was becoming more acidic than I had hoped it would. And so early on as well. Here we were having not seen one another in well over a decade, and without missing a beat I find myself once again trying to slow dance with a cactus plant. But hell and goddamn, I hadn't come all this way back to DC to leave with nothing for nothing.

"And what about 'Doc Hollow?'" I asked straight out. "What about that? Odd bit of noise, don't you think?"

This gave him a start.

"Sorry?"

"*Doc Hollow*. That mean anything to you, Walter?"

"Where…where did you hear that?"

"Little birdies."

"Indeed."

"Do you make anything of it?"

"I'm sure I don't know," he said looking away toward the window. "I have a patient who calls me Admiral Sherman and greets me with a salute every third Tuesday of the month. This is the business we're in, lad. Sick people will say the damnedest things."

"So you think it's a name then? 'Cause I'm not really certain. Not entirely."

"Where have you heard this?" he asked, clearly edgy. "I would really like to know."

"It's like I'm saying, Doc, just here and there."

"You've been calling on some of my patients, haven't you?" I suspect that he meant it to sound accusatory, but there was a sheepishness to his tone, as if I'd discovered some embarrassing bit of clutter in his closet.

"I'd...uh...I'd like to think of them as my patients too," I replied.

"Ah. I see. With whom have you visited? Where have you been?"

"West Virginia, Kentucky, Western Pennsylvania...stopped in Ashburn to—"

"So we have been a busy bee." Pause, then, "You...You went to Ashburn?"

"I did."

"Well I'll be..."

He seemed surprised, and perhaps even a bit unsettled by this piece of news. I realized then I had neglected to ask Salvador our boilerplate questions about Doctor Freeman, and I wondered how long it had been since he had come to visit his single greatest success.

"Sal sends his best," I said with a broad smile.

"And what of this Chris Williams?" Doc Freeman asked.

"What of him?"

"Did he go along with..." he tossed his hand as if waving away flying dust. "Bah. I suppose it doesn't much matter. *He* doesn't matter, that much is sure."

"I'd like to talk to that kid if I could, Walter. The kid from back when. Joseph Brinkley. Is he still alive?"

"*Of course* he's alive. And he is fine. I just spoke with his father last week. He's doing odd jobs, I hear."

"Can I meet him?"

"The Brinkleys wish to be left alone, lad. Respect their wishes."

"Do you still do it, Walter?"

"Do I still do what?"

"The transorbital."

I saw him visibly tighten up. He looked back at me with the same angled squint.

"The procedure has largely fallen out of favor of late. However, I still stand by it. It is solid medicine."

"Of course."

"So lad…how are we sleeping these days?"

"Like a baby."

"Is that so? No more sleep paralysis? No more late-night near-suffocation?"

"I didn't say a *healthy* baby."

"Go on."

"Some nights aren't so bad. It's definitely worse in DC, for some reason. Worse than anywhere else. It's an odd thing…but that's life, right?"

"You're going to die without treatment, you know."

"What sort of treatment is there?"

"For the paralysis, not much of anything. For the breathing, there is a surgery. It's new, but it seems to yield positive results for most people. They can cut out the back of your throat. Open up your air passages."

"Why is that always your solution, Walter? Just carve out the offending tissue. It's a strange first response for a neurologist, isn't it?"

"Tell me," he said turning, suddenly very interested, "is it *always* paralysis?"

"I'm sorry?"

"Do you suppose you might possibly also be a somnambulist?"

"A sleepwalker?"

"However you like it."

"I…don't know. I kinda doubt I'd have both. Right? The two syndromes pretty well cancel each other out…don't they? And why do you ask?"

"I'm just curious. I've always been fascinated by what a man might be capable of when he's unconscious. It's an oddly liberating notion, don't you think? That your sleeping self may have this whole other life independent of you."

"Why Doc, that's nearly Freudian of you."

"Very funny, lad. And I think you mean Jungian. But what I mean is your *physical* self, of course."

"I'm pretty sure my sleeping self is just trying not to choke to death. What are you getting at, Walter?"

"Stand up, please."

"Why?"

"Indulge me." We both stood. I fiddled with my pockets awkwardly as Freeman finally put his glasses back on his face and walked over to me. He put his hands on my face, and a small shiver betrayed me. With both thumbs he pulled down both of my lower eyelids. I began to sweat down my neck. I'd seen those hands do too much to not be a little unnerved.

"Still?" he said, peering into my eyes. "Still with the Thorazine? I'm amazed you're not suffering from tardive dyskinesia."

"Call it luck."

"You're starting to get a bit of the Shuffle, lad. You realize that, don't you? I noticed it when you first walked in."

They call it the Thorazine Shuffle. It's not a hot new dance craze on *American Bandstand*...but it sure as fuck should be.

"I'm 38 years old, Doc," I said. "I think you can stop calling me 'lad' now."

Freeman smiled, patted me on the cheek, and walked over to the Southside window overlooking the grounds.

"Fair enough," he said. "Fair enough. I'm no longer a young man, either. Nor particularly healthy, alas."

"What does that mean?"

I played dumb, but I knew how sick he was, and how much of a secret he was trying to keep it. He was, at the end of the day, my friend. And if I were inclined to have normal, human feelings I likely would have felt very sad for him. Thankfully I had well taken care of that horseshit.

For nearly a minute we didn't speak. He stared out the window across campus, searching for something that wasn't out there. I looked about the office, feeling no longer at home there. A stranger.

"You know, it's funny," he said finally, not answering my

question, "I have not performed a transorbital lobotomy in well over a year…but today, I am consulting a young woman concerning her eldest son. Dr. Chipman's wife, actually. If you can believe that."

"Dennis Chipman?" I asked. "The head shrinker?"

"The very same."

"He's a good man."

"Of course. A credit to his field to be sure."

"What's the problem with their boy?"

"Violent mood swings. Clear signs of severe manic depression. She is insisting upon a prefrontal. Really won't hear of anything else. Can you imagine? The wife of a clinical psychologist. But she's going behind his back to secretly meet with Walter Freeman. She thinks I am the only one who can save her son. It really is a funny thing."

"How old is the boy?" I asked. Silence. "How old is the boy, Walter?"

"That's confidential information."

"No it is not."

"Only Walter Freeman can save the boy…" he said, to himself and the window. "Only Walter Freeman…"

"Doc…hello?"

"The only one…"

"Walter…Walter?"

"Well," he said, snapping back to reality, "she should be here any moment. She's actually a bit late." He cleared his throat and straightened his vest sharply. "It was good to see you. Don't be a stranger, yes? No sense waiting another thirteen—"

"Just a minute, Doc. I need to ask you—"

And with that the door to the office flew open. *And in she walked*…a High Society Dame if ever I had seen one. Straight from the glossy pages. Conservative and prim, yet still dressed to the nines. Only the wealthy can pull that shit off.

But I recognized her right away. *You want fuck? Vill cost.*

For the moment, I was locked in place.

"I am *so* sorry to keep you waiting, Doctor Freeman," she said, ever so slightly out of breath. She had not even a trace of an accent about her voice. "It has been a rare day. This new maid of ours, god bless her, she barely speaks a word of English, and is simply a—" She stopped short at the sight of me. "Oh...my..."

I saw it in her eyes—*How to play this?* I could see her mulling over the option of pretending she didn't know me. Or perhaps trying to think of a reasonable lie to act out for Freeman, and hope I'd be game for it. Silently, wordlessly, she pleaded with me not to expose her. Not to blow her cover. Not to draw attention...not to draw attention...

It turned out to be needless worry, as Walter seemed thoroughly oblivious to the sudden shock and tension buzzing in the air.

"Fret not, Mrs. Chipman," he said, cool and professional. "Please do come in and have a seat." He turned to me and said, "We'll talk soon, yes?"

"Sure," I said, numbly shaking his hand. "Sure thing. I'll see ya. See ya 'round."

I didn't look at Irina as I left, but I thought I felt her eyes on me as I shut the door.

CHAPTER 20

I left Dr. Freeman's office even less sure of everything.

For three days I holed up in the cheapest hotel room I could find trying to reach Chris in Poughkeepsie by telephone. To no avail. We had planned to rendezvous in DC after I met with Freeman, but Chris was nowhere to be found. Nowhere he would normally be. Called and called and called and called, and nothing. *What the hell is going on?* I thought. And I wondered…if somebody might just be playing me for a chump.

So I simply hung about, waiting, pondering…with my medicine supply running low. I, of course, had keys to George Washington University, and knew the floors blindfolded. I could get into their stock with relative ease. But at that point I would officially be breaking and entering.

Just as I had at Walter's office, I felt like a stranger in DC, a town that I had always considered home. Since I was an orphan. Since forever. I doubt that I ever really belonged, bouncing around as I did, but I surely did not now. But by this time I could hardly navigate myself around the city. As if everyone had shifted all the furniture while I was away.

On the third night, cabin fever overtook me, and I had to get out.

I made a crawl through some of my favorite, familiar old haunts. I found some of them frozen in time, and some nearly unrecognizable of late. I couldn't decide which bothered me more.

Down on 18th and Columbia I settled in at Frank's Place, long-time my dive of choice back when. I'd always liked this area of town (which they were now calling Adams-Morgan), close as it is to Dupont Circle where I used to live for a time some years ago. I always liked the neighbors in that area, Mexicans for the most part, folks always ready and eager to throw some dice and drain a few bottles. My kind of crowd.

In the time since I had last been around, somebody had loaded the jukebox at Frank's with old jazz records, and this night some sad character must have dropped every coin he hand to his name on old Duke Ellington sides. They played all through the night, one after the other. It was almost enough to keep my mind off the fact that I had just shot up the last of my juice. Almost. I sat in the corner pouring whiskey down my throat, wondering why on god's gray earth I was there.

I saw Irina enter the bar, but I pretended that I did not. I watched her out of the corner of my eye as she eased past the ripped pool tables, pensive and unsure. Slowly she approached my table, and our eyes finally met.

"Hi there," she said with a little wave.

"*Gamarjoba*," I replied.

She smiled. I indicated the vacant seat.

"Thanks," she said, sitting, still wearing her dark, velvet swing coat. It was too dim inside the joint to see much of what else she was wearing, but it appeared to be a more sensible get-up for the joint than what she'd had on days before when I saw her in Doc Freeman's office. Here was a chick who knew how to play her surroundings on their terms. Smart all the way.

"Hey," she said. "Hi. Hi there. How are you? So...yes. I thought I might find you here."

"Yeah?"

"These used to be my stamping grounds too, right?"

She shouted over to the bartender, "Gin and...just gin. Double. On the rocks. Thank you."

"You could stay awhile," I said.

Without standing, she peeled the coat from her shoulders and draped it over the back of her chair. As casually as I could, I scoped out her bare arms. Just in case. They were smooth and clear, and I breathed a little sigh of relief, even though she never took the needle in her arms anyway.

"I have to say," she said, attempting a chuckle, "you gave me quite a shock the other day."

"Right back atcha, doll."

The bartender brought her drink to her.

"Keep them coming," she said to him indicating both of our glasses.

"You got it, sweetheart," he said, heading back to his station.

"Where have you been all these years?" she asked me.

"Do you really want to know?"

"I don't suppose I do, do I." She took a deep drink. "Duke Ellington, right?" she said, bobbing her head lightly to the music.

"You know I love it."

"I know you do."

"You've certainly done well for yourself," I said. "That's really great to see."

"I'm not normally accustomed to sneaking around behind my husband's back. Believe that or not."

"That's what I've heard."

"I'm sorry?"

"I like Dennis," I said, then corrected myself. "Dr. Chipman. He always showed me a lot of courtesy and respect. I can't say that for a lot of the doctors I've known. But he was always a stand-up fella. How did you meet?"

"Do you really want to know?"

I did not. "Touché," I said.

We clinked glasses and gulped. She didn't flinch, clearly a more experienced drinker than when last we met.

"So…forgive me for prying," I said, "but what's going on with your boy?"

"We have three boys," she said.

"The oldest. You know what I mean."

"Dennis would be horrified to find out I've been secretly meeting with Walter Freeman. Walter Freeman, of all people. But I'm at the end of the end of the end of my rope. Our son…Julien…God save me. He has kicked me, bitten me, scratched me, he pulls my hair, he has sprained my left wrist, broken three of my toes…I can't take it anymore. There's only one solution. I wish there was some other way, but—"

"Please don't do it," I interrupted.

"What?"

"Just trust me. Please don't. Whatever is wrong with your son, ripping open the front part of his brain with an ice pick is not the cure. No more than a bullet would be."

This got her back up.

"You don't know what it's li—…" she paused for a moment, reconsidered what she was about to say, then continued slowly. "OK, I know you probably see a lot worse every day…at the asylums…but it's not…not your child doing it."

"All the more reason NOT to do what you're planning," I said. "Please listen to me. You will not find a more expert opinion than the one you're getting right here and now. Do. Not. Do. This. If you love your son, you won't do it."

She looked at me and drank her gin, but did not answer.

"Do you know," I pressed further, "why Freeman hasn't performed a transorbital since February of last year? Do you? Would you like to wager a guess?" She did not respond, but studied her ice instead. "It's because he has been officially banned from operating. Ever again. And that's for life…not that he'll listen. His last patient, after her *third* lobotomy, died of a massive brain hemorrhage."

She nodded, but remained silent. We sat for a bit, drinking, listening to Duke's orchestra wail and rumble and sway through aging speaker cones.

"I've thought about you a lot over the years," she said finally.

"A lot."

"Me, too," I said truthfully. "Me, too. Isn't that weird?"

"It is, I guess. But…not really."

"Well, I mean we had a…"

"Go ahead. You can say it."

"A *professional* relationship."

"Yeah. I know…"

"And there's nothing wrong with that."

"I've…worried sometimes about you. I've felt guilty. Sometimes."

"*You* guilty?"

What the fuck for? I thought. *I'm the one who…*

"I feel guilty sometimes," she said again.

"You shouldn't. Not hardly."

I debated internally about letting it go, but decided to come out and ask anyway.

"You're not still…still on the needle, are you?"

"No no," she laughed. "Are you kidding? A gal like me? We don't do that along the upper crust."

"Outta sight," I said, breathing a sigh of relief. "Good. That's good to hear." And it was.

This was the longest I had gone in several years without any Thorazine, and I found myself becoming increasingly aware of the cool little trickles of actual human feeling that began to drip from the stalactites inside me. I did not particularly like it. But…I did like being there. With her.

"No," she said, "none of that for me. Instead I cuddle in bed with Sir Valium and Lady Merlot. They're a lovely couple and they know how to touch me just right."

She paused, and looked down at her ice. Swirling it around she said, "I…I've worried about you sleeping alone. Not being able to breathe, hoping and praying that someone would wake you. Worried that there'd be nobody there…"

"Well," I said, "I'm still here." *More or less.*

"You're a scary sleeper," she said. "I remember that. A scary, violent sleeper. You scared me a lot. I always wondered if you were capable of hurting people in your sleep without knowing it. I mean, besides yourself."

"What the hell?"

"Silly, I know," she said, shrugging it off. "It's not really that weird, you know."

"What's not weird?"

"That we have thought about one another over these last years. It's really not weird at all."

"Oh?"

"We were young. We were both so young. You need to understand...I mean...*this is DC*. All my...all my...*clients*...they were just...old, ugly and square. Politicos. Senators...staffers...presidential aides...the occasional jilted Washington wife. Old, boring, ugly and square. And I know it was like that for you too. In your world. We were both children, alone in a world of old men. I mean hell, you're STILL the lad!"

"True enough."

"I may have been on the street...but I was still a young girl. I wanted to have *fun*. I wanted to have friends. You were fun. More so than what I was used to. You were my friend...even if I wasn't yours."

This was all just a little too close. My skin started to prickle, and I could feel the first light, early jabs of withdraw.

"Irina..." I said. "I was a wreck. I was just as much a wreck then as I am now. I was just a younger wreck."

"Like hell," she said firmly. "You were a superhero! You were saving the world, remember? Like Jesus."

"Yeah...I guess...Now I don't know who to save. Or how. Or why."

"I love my life now," she said. "I love my husband. I love my kids. I'm very happy now..."

"I'm happy that you are."

"But...I miss the wild side. I miss the wild nights." She took my hand across the table. "*Menatrebi.*"

Menatrebi. I miss you.

"I've missed you too," I said.

"You want to save somebody?" she said, squeezing my hand and looking right into my eyes, desperate and yearning, "save *me*."

"From what? You're in the high life now. What could be better?"

"Save me," she pleaded. "Save me. And save yourself too."

"Are we in danger?" She didn't answer, but her eyes began to water. "It'll be OK," I said. *But what the fuck do I know.*

"You can still be the hero," she said. "It's not too late to be the hero."

"OK."

"I'm sorry," she sniffled, wiping the dampness from her eyes on the back of her hand. Her mascara smeared slightly. I liked it. I didn't know what the problem was, or what she thought I could do about it. But I figured I could be there for her all the same.

"Promise me you won't bring Julien to Dr. Freeman," I said. "Please. Promise me." Once again she didn't reply, but she held my hand tighter. And there we sat.

Suddenly, from out of the ether, the instrumental version of one of the Duke's greatest compositions began to play. We both smiled in recognition, and I couldn't help but sing to her—

"*Cigarette holder / which wigs me / over her shoulder / she digs me / out cattin' / that Satin Doll…*"

She blushed, giggling, "Aren't we just a little bit too young to be so terribly old?"

"*Baby shall we go / out skippin'? / Careful amigo / you're flippin' / Speaks Georgian / that Satin Doll…*"

I stood up and silently asked for her hand.

"I don't do this," she said. "I…I never do this."

I didn't budge, and she stood up and stepped out to a little clear spot on the floor with me. I took her right hand with my left. She put her left hand on my shoulder and I held her at the waist. We danced close. She rested her head on my chest and closed her eyes. When the verse came around, she sang softly—

"Telephone numbers / well you know / Doin' my rhumbas / with uno / and that n' my Satin Doll..."

We danced through the next several numbers without a word. And then, as *Warm Valley* began to fade in, she looked up at me and whispered—

"*Kiss me.*"

"I...I don't know..."

"Please kiss me," she whispered in my ear, nibbling on my neck. "I want you to kiss me. I need to be kissed. Right now."

It didn't seem right. In fact, I knew that it wasn't. But I loved being close to her. She made me forget about, or at least ignore, the pain of Thorazine hunger that began to hack at me from within.

You want me to save you, Satin Doll? I thought. *Maybe you could save me too...*

I lowered my head slightly closer to her, but I couldn't help but to be hesitant. I knew her husband, after all. I liked and admired him. And even by the most charitable of standards, I'm a goddamn lowlife. Far below the class of man she should be with anymore.

Finally, she reached up, took control and kissed me hard.

"Come away with me to my secret place," she whispered, peppering my ear with kiss after kiss, "I have something to share."

CHAPTER 21

"Where are we?"

We had walked several blocks to get there, through a part of town I was not familiar with. Or did not remember. Mostly industrial. Empty lots. All stone, glass and gravel. Bent steel girders and barbed wire fencing.

We ducked down an alley, pushed through an open door, and headed up two flights to an old warehouse space. Cardboard boxes, a few old chairs, hubcaps and discarded pieces of sheet metal hanging from steel racks. Dank, dark, coated in oily shadows. No windows. It was not a particularly romantic locale.

"My secret hiding spot," she said smiling and breathing deeply, as if she finally felt at home.

"Back in the old days," she said, "when I was in trouble, or someone was chasing me, or what have you, I would run here and hide. I still come here to be alone sometimes. Even now. *Especially* now."

She gave a little Cinderella twirl, her arms outstretched, as if we were standing in a lush green field.

"Sometimes I just don't want to be found," she said, "do you know what I mean?"

"I do indeed."

"Perfect secret place to bring my secret friend," she said with a wink and a swing of her hips.

"All right, then."

She fell into my arms and planted a hard smooch on me, in the process pushing me down into one of the chairs.

"Have you missed me?" she said. "Tell me that you've missed me."

"I have. Sure I have."

"I can't all the time play the Good Mommy/Good Wifey role," she said, a bit of her old accent finally seeping through. "I'm just not so good an actress."

She kicked off her high heels, reached under her skirt and pulled her panties down, kicking them unceremoniously to the side and across the cold, smooth warehouse floor. She didn't bother with anything resembling seduction, or foreplay, as the grimy atmosphere and clandestine nature of the moment seemed enough for her. All she needed to get the engine revving. She straddled me, undid my belt, and unzipped my fly.

"I want you to want me," she whispered, gnawing at my ear, "I *vont you to vont be deep inside me.*"

"Been a while...has it, doll?"

"You haff no idea."

And with that, I was indeed inside her.

She seemed to relish the control of being on top, using me as a static device for her pleasure, which was more than fine with me. She stared hard into my eyes, panting and mewling, biting her lips (and mine), gripping my upper arms with both hands, pressed against the back of the chair. I could feel myself building to climax, but I held off, as she pumped harder and faster.

At one point I thought I saw her look past me, but she quickly focused her gaze upon me even more directly.

"What is it?" I asked.

"*Nuss*—...Nothing," she panted, "Fuck me...Keep fucking me..."

I was just along for the ride, so I continued to let her use me however she liked. She clamped her fingers around both of my arms and the backrest of the chair like vice grips.

"I'm going to come soon…" she said in a clipped whimper. "Gonna come…gonna come…"

And then suddenly, I was grabbed from behind by several black-gloved hands.

"What the fuck?!"

In a flash my arms, head, and chest were all restrained as I fought and lost against my invisible captors. Irina jumped off of me and began quickly gathering up her shoes and underwear.

"Oh god!" she screamed. "Don't hurt him!"

"IRINA!" I tried to yell, but the sleeve of a black, plastic rain jacket muffled my voice.

"I'm sorry!" she cried. "I'm so sorry! I never wanted to hurt you! I had no choice! He threatened my family! Please forgive me!"

And just like that, she ran off.

"Irina! IRINAAAAAAAAAAAAAAA!!!"

I struggled to get free as the figures tied my arms behind the chair. The rope burned against my wrists, sawing through my skin, blood pouring hot down my fingers. I swung my head back, hoping to make contact with the bridge of a nose, but it was no use. All went dark as my head was enveloped in a black hood. I could hear them all around me, murmuring eerily, chattering in some unintelligible gibberish.

"What do you want?!" I hollered, which was all but swallowed up by the hood and the noise. I heard clanging and clattering, as if they had all begun banging the hubcaps and sheet metal with no discernable rhythm. Inside the hood I could barely catch a breath, and the sweat began to pour from my face.

"WHAT THE FUCK DO YOU WANT?!?!" I screamed.

A hand clamped down on the top of my head, and I heard a voice slur into my ear—"Doc…Hollow'lllll…be 'ere soonnnn…"

And with that I felt the dull *whack* of what was likely my own blackjack against the back of my skull. The pain pierced my brain, and inside the pitch black of the hood silent fireworks exploded all around me.

But it did not knock me out.

I supposed that was the intention, however, so I slumped my head forward, pretending unconsciousness. The cacophony grew louder as I heard the voice say again, although likely not to me—
"Doc…Hollow'lllll…be 'ere soonnnn…"

PART THREE
LADIES AND GENTLEMEN…
DOC HOLLOW

I take one last look over my shoulder. Feel the burn in my lungs. Yep, they're chasing me. Again.

"Ain't no use in runnin'!" the lead boy screams at me, his gang alongside him. Arthur is his name. "Just makin' it harder on yourself when we catch ya. And we will catch ya!"

Not again. No you won't.

If only outrunning bastards was an Olympic event, I'd be going for the gold.

"Yer dead when we catch ya!"

Not this time, you mother fucker.

A week earlier he buried his hammy fist in my stomach, taking with it my wind and my lunch. We're not doing that again.

"Stop now and we won't thrash you!"

I'll take that bet.

I catch my reflection in a storefront window. I look to be about twelve or so. It must be 1942, or in that neighborhood. I'm not watching my front, and I run head on into some fat swell in a shiny new suit.

"Watch it, you little urchin!" He shouts, grabbing me by the collar.

"Sorry, mister, it was an accident! Honest!"

"Have you no sense? What is the matter with you?"

"I...I..."

"OK, boy, be truthful now," he says squinting with badger eyes right down in my face. "What's your line? Pickpocket are you?"

"N-no, sir," I stammer, "Those guys back there, they w-were chasing me."

"Likely story."

"It's the truth!"

"No discipline, that's the problem. Your father ought to take the belt to you. Warm you up something proper."

"I ain't g-got a father. Or a mother."

"Well that explains it, doesn't it? My son's off fighting in Guadalcanal so filthy little animals like you can run wild in the streets. Eh? Eh?!"

I quit squirming, trying to plan a way out of this pickle. He's too big for me to fight, and if I swing on him the police will be on my tail in a blink. And it's a cinch then that the brothers at old Saint Joe will be sure to give me the business if they have to come collect me from the police station. Again. I'll likely not sit down again for the rest of my days.

"Excuse me, good sir," we hear Arthur say behind us, in a tone too dandy by half, "This wretch here is a fugitive from St. Joseph's Orphanage." The ratfink walks boldly toward us with an air that is not at all harmonious with his shabby, tattered outfit. "If you'll let me escort him back home, he's got a good and proper lashing waiting for him there." Arthur clamps his right mitt down on my shoulder with a broad grin.

Satisfied that I have what's coming to me, the man releases me, grunts approval, and shuffles on his way.

"Let's walk nicely now," Arthur hisses through his teeth. "Shall we?"

Flanked on all sides by the bastard and his toughs, I walk through the crowded streets like a crook to the gallows. Serves me right, after all. I let myself get sloppy. Pretend for one second like the world isn't out to get you, and that's exactly when it lays you out with a sucker punch.

"Spose I should thank you, eh, Artie?" I chuckle bitterly. He guffaws in reply, and the boys do likewise. And we keep marching. I know we'll be clear of prying eyes soon, and they'll lay a whipping on me. So it's time to bargain. "I don't suppose if I just give you my last nickel now we can call it square?"

"Pay up right now…and we'll *see* about what's what," Arthur says, never easing up on his crocodile smile.

I pull the coin out of my pocket as we continue walking along, careful not to make a big show amidst all the bustle. The sunlight catches it nice and shiny as I begin to hand it over to him. He extends his left hand, and just as I'm about to drop it in, I tuck it into my palm with my right middle finger, grab his left hand and shove it into the coat pocket of the towering Swede walking one step in front of us.

"THIEF!!!" the man bellows, swinging backward with a brick-thick fist, which I duck, and bashes ol' Artie right across the puss. And I'm gone like a shot.

I double back around the corner and hide in the doorway of a newer tenement. I watch as they hunt for me, splitting off in groups of two, peeking around corners, talking to dirty faced men, holding their hands at head height, I can only assume asking if anybody has seen me. All they get in return are shoves and shaking heads. Exactly what they deserve.

Say what one might about Arthur—and I would say plenty— for a boy of lower intelligence and little real purpose here on Earth, he's tenacious if nothing else. And, depending on how you look at it, either he's extremely lucky or I got the luck of a leper, because as I laugh silently at them and plot my exit, I fail to notice that the gate in front of the alley is shut and covered in chains and locks. Artie and the boys have unknowingly cornered me again, and if I so much as cough, I'll be found out and pounded stupid.

There's nowhere to go from here. I squeeze myself into a

corner shadow, hoping to blend into the soot and stone, and try to hold my heavy breaths so as not to give myself away. The clomping of their gunboats against the street grows closer. I can hear them chinning amongst themselves, grumbling about, "*Which way'd he go?*"

"Hey, what are you fellas looking for?"

I could spot that voice anywhere, and wager she saw me duck for cover. She was likely off hiding herself nearby, reading a book or writing in that diary of hers.

She's a swell gal…what's her name? Ethel? Edna? Edith? I'm pretty sure it's Edith.

I'm sure she won't blow my cover…will she? *What if they bribe her?* Hey, things are tough all over. And all us kids at St. Joseph's, we know from tough. Arthur and company are willing to shake me down for my last nickel, after all. What would they do for real money?

"So you seen him or what?" Arthur asks her, leaning in like a real tough character, still rubbing his aching jaw. She just shrugs and snaps her chewing gum.

"Might have," she says, wrinkling up her freckled nose like she's giving it a serious thought. "I seen lotsa things today."

Girl's got cheek, I'll give her that. Must be that Irish blood.

"You're wastin' time, skirt. Whaddaya want?"

"I don't want nothing but my fair share," she says. "'Cause I happen to know he's got a whole dollar stuffed in his left shoe." Well you can bet those greedy thugs are getting the wide-eyes now. "He's secretly a rich man, and I'll bet you didn't know."

Funny. That's awfully funny. I haven't seen a dollar since I can remember, much less stuff one in my shoe. But ol' Edith, she knows the right words to say. I about can't believe it myself, opening my eyes and peeking around just so, when I see Arthur pull a shiny dime from his pocket and drop it in her hand!

"Now sing, birdy," he growls, really laying on the act.

"He's hiding in the chapel," she says, pointing back toward St. Joseph way. "Or he will be soon. That's where he's headed.

That's where he always goes to hide. Betchas didn't know that neither. Prolly in the sacristy, if I don't miss my guess."

The lot of them all dart off back toward the chapel without another word.

With the coast clear I come out from the shadow.

"Thanks for the cover," I say, dusting myself off.

"Wasn't much of nothing, really," she says casually. "Close shave, huh?"

"I've had closer," I say, still catching my breath.

"You skinned yourself a bit," she says, wetting her thumb with her tongue and wiping a spot of blood from my chin. I can tell by the look in her eyes that I'm likely streaked with coal dust and sweat.

"Hey," I say, "I never claimed to be a pretty face, now did I."

She grins in spite of herself, looking down at the ground, her pale cheeks toasting up nice and pink.

"We'd do well to shake a leg," she says. "After Father Brinkman's through tanning their hides for busting into the chapel, they'll be out for blood."

"I'll say they will."

"We've got a whole fifteen cents between us," she says with a wink.

"Let's paint the town then!"

I buy her a Coca-Cola with my last nickel as a thank-you for helping me dodge ol' Artie. She shares it with me. It's a fine little moment between us. A kiddie romance, without too much in the way of grown-folk clutter. She's a cute little thing, but not too far out of my league. She smiles, blushes, and looks away. I do too.

Just as she's taking her last swallow she perks up suddenly, her eyes brightening. She grabs my hand and we go running from the drugstore and on down the alley.

"Can't you hear it?" she says, "Oh, it's so beautiful!"

I have no idea what she's on about, but we keep on running, trying not to trip over jagged cobblestones. At a point she lets go of my hand and darts ahead.

"Hey, wait up!" I shout.

As we round a corner back into the open air I hear a voice crooning:

"*Round my Indiana homestead waves the cornfields / In the distance loom the woodlands clear and cool / Often times my thoughts revert to scenes of childhood / Where I first received my lessons / nature's school...*"

I find her standing in front of a stoop where a young Negro man sits singing, his eyes closed.

"*But one thing there is missing from the picture / Without her face it seems so incomplete / I long to see my mother in the doorway / As she stood there years ago, her boy to greet...*"

"I love this song," she whispers, her eyes wet with tears.

I don't much care for old Tin Pan Alley tunes. But as those things go this is a fine one, and the man has a swell voice. As he sings further, the tears begin to spill down her freckled cheeks, burning them red with salt.

"*Oh, the moonlight's fair tonight along the Wabash / From the fields there comes the breath of new-mown hay / Through the sycamores the candle lights are gleaming / On the banks of the Wabash, far away...*"

"Thank you," she says to the young Negro, sniffling, and drops the dime she had scammed from Arthur into his flopped leather cap setting on the ground.

"Thank *you*, Miss," he says, never once looking up at her. Without a beat missed he launches into another song, and we go about our way.

We shuffle on toward the West End in silence, the shouting of pushcart vendors echoing from somewhere near New Hampshire Avenue and 21st Street. Finally she says, "Wasn't that a wonderful song?"

"I'll say it sure was."

"My grandmamma used to sing that to me. We used to live in Indiana. Near the Wabash."

"How do you know? You been at St. Joseph's since you're a

year old."

"I just know."

"And how did you get from Indiana to Washington DC anyhow?"

"*I just know.*"

"All right then."

"That fellow back there," she says, pointing backward with her thumb, "He sings every Saturday night at the Jungle Inn up in Shaw."

"How do you know *that*?" I ask. She gives me a wry smirk and keeps walking.

"Air sure is thick today," she says. "Let's walk to the river. At least there'll be a breeze."

At the bank we sit, and she rolls up her patchy dress and graying apron over her bare legs. There I can see she has stitched a number of good-sized pockets into the underside of the dress, perfect for stashing pilfered goods. From two of the pockets she pulls a green apple and a jar of peach preserves.

"Nicked 'em from the fruit cart," she says proudly, tossing the apple to me. I bite into its tight, tart skin ravenously.

"*Nyshly done*," I say, my mouth full of apple pulp.

"So tomorrow is the big old annual Prospective Parents Visiting Day," she says, cracking the lid on the preserves. "You nervous?"

"Why would I be?" I say, handing the apple back over to her. "Why should either of us? We are WAY too old to be adopted. That ship has long since sailed."

"I don't want to be adopted," she says. "I want to work. I want to be an apprentice. Gals are working now, you know."

"Just don't set yourself up," I say. "I mean, good luck and all. But don't go and get a broken heart."

"Talk about a ship that's long sailed," she says with a salty laugh. I nod and scoop out a bit of preserves with my fingers. The peaches are so sweet and sharp, they nearly cover the bitter ash and soot flavor from my fingertips. "What about you?"

"I wanna work," I say. "Real work. Not in St. Joseph's

laundry room. Something *important*. Save-the-world important, you know?"

"There's the police department," she says. "Lots of good Irish chaps there."

"I don't think I'm Irish. And anyway," I say deadpan, "then I'd have to bust you for a no-good thief."

"You'd never!" she squeals, punching my arm.

"Just doin' my job, ma'am."

"You could be a doctor," she says. "We always need more doctors. Especially when all the Johnny's come marching home, hurrah hurrah."

"Yeah" I say, "maybe I could at that."

We stare out across the Potomac as the setting sun spills a cascade of blood-orange across the ripples. The breeze is cool, and right now, everything's just fine. I look over at the girl sitting next to me. *I think her name is Edith.* But even though it's 1942, and we're both twelve years old, I know that in seven years' time this girl will be strapped down on a gurney at Rockland State Hospital and they'll fry her brain with electricity. Because she's "hysterical." And that's *after* one of Doc Freeman's disciples cuts open her frontal lobe. Because she's "hysterical." It won't go well. There will be complications.

And those toughs who were chasing me? Arthur and his gang? Two of them will die in prison. The rest will die in Korea. I'm the only one of us who sees thirty years old.

And I really thought I had come out ahead. But as the sun sets, and the scene along the river fades to pitch black, and the girl and the grass and the world disappear, and the cool breeze is replaced by the stifling heat of this black hood that I'm suffocating inside, I hear the sound of murmuring, jabbering dead-eyed lunatics banging on sheet metal somewhere just beyond my throbbing head, and now I'm not so sure. I'm not so sure.

At some point the hood was pulled from my head. Relieved as I was to be able to breathe again, I was struck by the dank, cold atmosphere of the room. Despite the temperature, though, my perspiration increased, and I felt nauseous from mounting withdraw.

Through the dim light and my fuzzy vision I could see the figures, jittering, some flapping their limbs like distressed waterfowl. The faces that weren't obscured by rain jacket hoods were still blurry to me, but in what little I could make out, they looked utterly empty. All of them. Skeletal in their lack of expression.

My throat felt like Arizona and the back of my head pounded from where the one had taken a loose blackjack to me. I wasn't sure why I wasn't dead. I wasn't so sure that I wasn't dead, except for the assumption that Hell would be more specific than this.

I closed my eyes and tried to will myself back to the Potomac at sunset, but I couldn't get past the reality of that girl being long dead. Whatever her name was. Neither could I not face the pathetic realization that even my fondest memories were knotted up in a blanket of hopelessness and despair. But that could have just been the withdraw talking. The lack of Thorazine was really starting to chomp away on me, and I knew that as the craving grew, the emotions that it normally suppressed for me would come barreling down the pipeline in a blithering rage. I feared that more than the pain. Or these jabbering psychotics, whoever they were. Much more.

Suddenly, the figures became even more agitated as a trio of them came bursting in, dragging another hooded victim. It was a man, for sure, tall and lanky. After they tied him to the chair beside me, they backed away, as if he might detonate. Some shorter figure ran up and yanked off the hood, then scurried quickly away.

"Chris!"

"Oh god, oh god," Chris said, in full blanched-out panic. "What…what is happening?!?!"

The addition of the new person to the space seemed to send a few of them over the edge, and for several long moments the raincoated figures shook, slammed, and pounded on scrap metal and old hubcaps, chattering and humming in some alien tongue. We could only sit, terrified, struggling to get free. And failing.

"Been in a trunk..." Chris said, panting, "seven hours...at least...they grabbed me...outside Riverside..."

"Are you OK?"

"As well as you," he said.

"That's not good."

"Not at all."

We tried to laugh. All the while, the clanging, banging, and dark muttering continued. I saw a trickle of blood coming down the side of Chris's long, pointed face, and I assumed that they had tried to blackjack him too.

And then...I saw it, oozing out of the darkness of the warehouse, a large, dark, bedraggled figure, looking like a young Rasputin with a blank, rounded face and a black raincoat. Empty as the rest, but more *dead*. His eyes were nothing but small, dark caverns against the white granite of his face. He also appeared to be having difficulty controlling his motor-functions: jerks, tics, and spasms in clockwork repetition.

"Morning-hmmmm...gennlem'n..." the phantom slurred in monotone, "I truss you're comfort'ble." I looked around to all the dark figures, and they shook and flapped all the harder. "Hmmmm...an' to think...it all started with the humble ice pick..."

"Doc Hollow, I presume," I said, defeated, my voice quivering just slightly. The Transorbitals murmured louder still, banging against anything in reach that made a piercing clatter.

"Why..." Chris said, shivering, near hysterics, "why do they have to do that?!"

The large figure bent his featureless, bearded face down to Chris and hissed through his tangled jungle of hair—

"Because-hmmmm...they are unable to screammm." He turned toward the assembled and asked, "Any-one here know this...Chris Williams-hmmm?"

A young, barely visible woman stepped forward, raising an unsteady hand. At this, The Transorbitals stopped banging, but continued to shake and murmur quietly.

"Lydia?" Chris said directly to the woman. "Lydia Jacobs! You know me! Lydia, it's me! Doctor Williams!" The girl did not respond. "Lydia, talk to me! How did you get here?! Tell me how you've been! Please come here!" She did not move. "It's Doctor Williams, Lydia! Please!"

"Go onnn home, Lydia," said Doc Hollow. "You are dis...missed. We'll give you a few-hmmm...moments."

The girl made her exit with a labored, faltering gait.

"No, Lydia, wait!" Chris shouted. "Please! Please come back!!!"

And like that, she was gone.

"Jig is prob'ly up after this one. Hmmm?" said Doc Hollow. "No walk'n away now. As you could likely tell by Bruce Haines, we've pritty mush lost int'rest in r'maining anonymousss."

"What's this all about, man?" I said, although I was pretty sure I knew already. To which Hollow and all of The Transorbitals replied in unison—

"MEDICINE."

With black plastic gloves on his hands, Doc Hollow pulled from his pocket a mallet and a leucotome. A bolt of frozen horror shot through me.

"Oh Jesus..." I said.

"You reco'nize this pick? Hmmmm?"

Of course I did. How could I not...

I nodded. "It's an orbitoclast."

"Freeman original," said Doc Hollow. "Won't break off in th' socket...like those old Ulines did. Who could know? Hmmm? It'ss an imprecise science aft'r all hmmmmmm."

Hollow handed the spike and the mallet to one of the other figures wearing an identical pair of black gloves.

"Oh god no...don't..."

"This iss how we save the world-hmmm..."

The remaining Transorbitals grabbed Chris Williams and leaned him back in the chair, securing his shoulders, legs, and head.

"No!" Chris screamed, struggling. "Please don't do this!"

"LET HIM GO!" I yelled.

I thrashed in my chair trying to get free. Somehow the knots seemed to grow tighter on my arms.

They pried Chris's eyes open, holding his head tight—just as I used to do. I tried to look away, but could not.

"OH GOD NO! PLEEEEASE NOOOOOO!" Chris shrieked.

"All bett'r soon, Dr. Will'ams," Hollow said, looking off, away from the scene. "All better soonnn…"

Powerless, I looked on in horror and Doc Hollow stood idly by as the pick was hammered straight into Chris's left eye. He screamed in agony as blood poured down his face, spurting across the cold warehouse floor.

I finally willed my eyes shut and turned away, but the sound of the hammering was even worse than the sight of it.

KNOCK—squish…KNOCK KNOCK KNOCK KNOCK… squish…

The screaming finally died away. Behind closed eyelids the room spun like a carnival ride, and I threw up down the front of my shirt.

"Why?!" I asked weakly, opening my eyes to slits, trying to keep from vomiting again. "He's dead, isn't he? He's dead. Why? WHY?!?!"

"Hmmmm…guess we need more practice…" he said.

"Why did he have to die?!"

Doc Hollow did not respond. He stood still, but for a slight shaking in his head. No words…Nothing…for nothing…Nothing…

I shut my eyes again, and the nausea increased. Even still I shook my head and hummed to myself, to block out the murmuring all around me.

I opened my eyes and they were all gone, as was Chris's body. All that was left in the warehouse was a pool of fresh blood, Doc Hollow, and me.

* * *

Hours passed. Hollow remained where he was, silently, going through a maddening pattern of repeated physical gestures. A jerk back of the head, a back left hand across the brow, three tics of the right shoulder. Over and over and over. And over again. I would try to speak to him. And he would not respond. I wasn't entirely sure he was aware that I existed anymore.

"Listen, fella," I said, shivering from fever and pouring cold sweat, "I don't know what it is you've got planned for me, or why…but I really need some fucking Thorazine." Nothing. "If it's some sort of information you want from me, my ability to lucidly give it to you is rapidly running out. I need Thorazine, now!"

Nothing from Hollow. Nothing…Nothing…

Jerk the head, hand across the brow, three tics. Jerk the head, hand across the brow, three tics. Jerk the head, hand across the brow, three tics. And nothing.

More hours passed. *And I'm dying*, I thought. I didn't know if it was true, or that I wanted it to be. I'd thrown up again, and I thrashed about so hard that I tipped my chair over. I lay on the freezing, glazed concrete of the warehouse floor, tied up and pressing on the nerves in my right shoulder in a way that shot bolts of pain through my entire body.

"PLEASE!!!" I screamed, "You gotta unnerstan', man, I've been shooting Thorazine for nearly twenty years! And I cannot go off it cold turkey! The withdraw shock could fucking kill me! IT COULD FUCKING KILL ME!!! If you're going to kill me anyway, then just stab me in the fucking head and GET IT OVERWITH! Just don't let me die like this!"

With that, he bent over and lifted me up into a proper sitting position again.

"I've never…hmmm…killed anyone in my life…" he said. "Annn' I nev'r will…huhhh…I merely…plant seeds…"

"Why are you doing this to me?!"

"I'm not…punish'ng you. I'm free'ng you. If it were poss'ble for me…to be tied to a chair…ann' sweat out MY lobotomy…I'd be etern'lly grateful…to the one who tied the knots."

I stared at his blank face, trying to jog my memory. If I could just place him, I thought, maybe we could talk. Really talk. Something in the shape of his cheeks was familiar, but the beard and the jungle of hair and the dead black eyes gave me nothing. For nothing.

"Doc-ter Freeman wouldn't hear that my procedure was not entirely a suc-cess," he said, the word *Freeman* spitting through clenched teeth. "Trotted me out in front of hisss colleagues like I'm a show pony, hmm. Stepmom wasn't hmmm…satisfied. They locked me up anyway."

Stepmom…stepmom…Goddamn it all…Should have known…I am so fucking stupid…

"I know you," I said. "I know who you are."

"Hmmmmmmm…" he nodded.

I thought it my only chance at survival to try to engage him person to person. As a human being. What other options were there? *Hail Mary, fulla grace, what do I have to lose…*

"Please listen to me," I said, as clearly as I could through the fear and withdraw shivers. "I want you to know, and this is for real, from my heart, and from deep in my soul…that *I am sorry*. I am so sorry. I was sorry then. I've been sorry every single day of my life since then. And I've thought about you every day. Every single fucking day, Joseph. Believe that I have. Every single day. Do you hear me, Joseph? Every single day."

At the sound of his own name, I thought I saw something lifelike flash across his cadaver eyes. But just as quickly as it had come, it was gone. He sat down across from me in Chris's now vacant chair, slumping awkwardly, like a vibrating corpse.

"Hmmm…You got time to hearrr a story, frien'?" he said. I watched as he struggled to enunciate his words, with varying degrees of success. "Why don't you sit a spell? Hmm?"

"Funny," I said. "That's funny, Joseph."

"Do you have the time to hear," he continued, "about the hell that my life hass beennn…has been…for twenny years…about what the in-stit-utions are like…from th' OTHER side? Hmmmm? When you're locked inside? Hmmmm? I've beennn made…made into a useless shell of a man. A ghost. A shadow. I'm a…burden to my family. And I'll hmmmm…never…ever…ever get any better. So…thank you for that."

"I'm sorry, Joseph…" I said, barely able to eke anything beyond a whisper. "Please believe me…I'm so sorry…"

I had heard similar stories to this one. The transorbital lobotomy did not empty the asylums, it created thousands of new patients. Permanently.

"Go on, Joseph. Tell me."

"Made some inter'sting discoveries in the bin, though," he said. "One for start…may…be 'cause I was so young…my brain adapted to what was damaged. Huh…Scar tissue grew 'round th' wounds."

"Yeah?"

"I could *think*."

"Good. That's good to hear, man. Good for you."

"Yes. Couldn't express…no focus at first…but I could think. Two," he held up two fingers to illustrate, "my fellow lobotomites were not terr'bly difficult to innn-fluence…or corral."

"Makes sense," I said.

"Three," he continued to hold up only two fingers, "and mos' cru-shuh…most crucial…doctors and staff, they un-der-est-im-ated us. They would. Always. Just as ever'one on the outside does now. Under-estim-ated."

"I understand. I surely do."

And I did. Or, I thought I did.

"You know when hospital staff fin'lly d'scovered we were sneaking out at night?" he said. "Hmmmm?"

"When?"

"When all the girls over innn D Quad…turned up pregn'nt."

With that he began to *laugh*…a harsh, staccato, machine-like sound, breaking through his slack, half-opened mouth. It went on for way too long, and I wasn't sure if he actually thought it was funny, or if he simply had no gauge of how long something like that should go on.

Eventually I joined him in the laugh. The barking sound of our laughter echoed thought the warehouse. In that moment, covered in my own sick, sweating out withdraw, with my dead friend's blood still glistening across the stone floor, the thought of a bunch of dead-eyed teenage lobotomites balling their little heads off after hours was the funniest goddamn thing I had ever imagined.

"Un-der-estimate us…" he continued, finally, "always…'til it's too late. Hmmmmm…"

"So you've been convincing former patients to kill doctors…but not their own doctor. Keep it random. No patterns. 'Accidents' and 'suicides.' Maintain alibis. And no one suspects…"

"No one s'spects invis'ble people," he said. "Pritty simple. We've been doing this…for jus' a bit lessss than a decade…"

"What? Less than a decade? But how can that be? These deaths have been happening—"

"The ones before us…really were random…'ccurrences…or somebody else'sss handi-work…Hmmmmm…"

"So why show your hand now?" I asked. "Why get sloppy?"

"Because the op'ration is…switch-ing focus. An' that'sss where you come in. Your time to shine."

And with that, he stood up and shuffled away. Left me alone, tied to a chair in a cold, damp warehouse stinking from vomit. Shaking and shivering. I didn't even bother to shout after him as he left. There was really no point to it. *We all have our lot in life. This is, apparently, mine.*

I had no idea how long he would be gone this time. I had no sense of how long I had been there already. The fever would flair; then subside. Flair again, and then subside. Just when I thought I was through the worst of it, it would spiral back again. I'd get the shakes, and then they'd ease up. Over and over.

As I sat, trapped, in the empty cavernous darkness of the warehouse, with no gauge of time and nothing but the maddening, endless, uncontrollable repetition of dull sensations cycling through me, I could not help but wonder...*Is this what it is like to live every day as a Transorbital?*

So...

I kept myself steady with a song. Just one, single song. I heard Ellington's orchestra play it live one time. In New York. I never found out who the singer was.

I cain't go out walkin' / ain't for no talkin' / baby done left me / just settin' and a-rockin'...

And so I sat and rocked and sang the song to myself.

Sittin' all day without holdin' my baby / I'm such a lonely papa / if she don't hurry and come back / I'm a cinch to blow my top-a...

It worked. It kept my mind distracted from my reality. The warehouse, the smell, the damp, dank air, the ache in my twisted arms and back, the piercing burn of the ropes against my wrists, it all faded into the background. No match for the lush horns and tinkling piano of the Ellington Orchestra.

And after a while...the velvet curtain opened, and the crowd clapped and cheered. And they danced close together as I crooned the tune, dandy and fine in my tailored new suit, and the boys all played that fine, mellow swing behind me. And it was fine. And everything was just fine. It kept the pain away. It kept the pain at bay. And we sounded great that night. We really sounded great. The crowd went wild.

If I had been schemin' / instead of dreamin'/ she never would have left me / just-a settin' here rockin' all day long...

Thunderous applause.

"Thank you, Ladies and Gentleman. Thank you so much for coming out tonight..."

1968, baby, all right? Outta sight. It's a new scene now. I've left the smoky old clubs behind, can you dig it? Here I am grooving high, like Bird called it, with all my far out, turned-on brothers and sisters in The Haight...or is it Greenwich?...saving the world one reefer at a time...freaking out to acid rock...(whatever that is)...Outta sight...yeah...outta sight...

The dope is free and the chicks are free and I'm free and everything's just fine...

...and that's how I know that this is only a dream. And since I'm aware of this fact, my mind forces itself awake and my eyes pop open.

But my body doesn't wake up.

I'm alone in a warehouse tied to a chair. Paralyzed and struggling to breathe. My head hangs low, cutting off what little air I can take in. No matter how hard I try, I cannot move. All I can see is the floor, and my vomit-stained lap.

Choke...choke...choke...Panicked and paralyzed...choke...choke...choked...

Dying...

Someone shakes me. Shakes harder. I finally awaken with a deep gasp of cold, stale air...and I SCREAM—

"AAAAAAAAAAAAAAAAAAAAAAAAAAAAAAAAAAAAAAHHHHHH!"

I see nothing but a violent gray blur streaking past my eyes. Shapeless and tumbling. We focus. Steady. Steady. Focus. And there he is.

"Turn'ng blue there hmmmmmm..."

"Yeah..." I wheezed and coughed, sputtering. "Uh huh...That does happen..."

"Thass no good, huhhhhhh."

"This..." I said, forcing in all the air I could grab, Hollow standing over me, his shaking hand still on my shoulder, "This is how..." I struggled to make the words leave my mouth, desperate as I was for more new oxygen. "This is how I'm going to die, Joseph...Ch—...choking in my sleep. Paralyzed."

"I won' let 'at happ'n," he said. He held a red, checkered thermos to my lips. Water. Cool and delicious. I sucked it down ravenously, feeling the soothing liquid fill every parched cell in my body.

"Hmmm…I'll stay awake," he continued, "…an' watch you. I'll wake you if…you're in d'stresss."

"What…" I said, still desperately dragging air into my burning lungs, but grateful for the drink of water, "what do you care?"

"I care."

"Why?"

"You're valu'ble to me."

"Bullshit," I said. "I'm not valuable to anyone."

"I know what you mean. Hmmm…"

"I'm really sick, man," I said. "I really need my medicine."

"Onna con-trary…you're almos' better. Gett-ing there."

"I could still go into shock, Joseph. Don't you understand that?"

"Thorazine's not physic'lly addictive…it jus' feels 'at way."

Yeah…there is that…

"OK, pal." Had my arms been free I would have thrown them up in resignation. "Whatever you say. You win."

"Tell me sump'n," he said, "Pal."

"Yeah?"

"You ev'r listen to Char-lie Parker?"

"What?"

"Charlie Parker. You are a fan at all? Hmm?"

"Are you fucking serious?"

"I'm a fan…" he said. "I think. Iss hard for me to unner'stannn music. But I like him."

"You don't say."

"Diff'rent people hear Bird in diff'rent ways."

"True enough."

"A lot of people juss hear a smooth sound…"

"They're not really listening then."

"Oth'rs hear a bunch of random, chaotic notes…"

"Yeah?"

"But what I hear?" He struggled to enunciate again. "I hear…violence. Hahhhhhh…I hear violence in his horn. It's those high toness. Tones. Jabbing…stabbing…piercing…That iss…that's what I hear from Char-lie Parker."

I will be damned...

"I hear that too, Joseph...Yeah, I hear it too. Sure. Sure I do. But not quite the same as you."

"Hmmmmm?"

"You know what I hear from Bird?" I said. "Huh? I hear him screaming out in pain through his horn. Screaming for help. And nobody ever helped him. Nobody. Ever. He died needing help that never came." I tipped my head back as I felt my eyes welling up with tears. They burned streaks down my grime-coated face.

Just the withdraw, you maudlin fool...

"Who coulda helped him?" he said with a bit more force than I had yet heard from him. His facial muscles twitched. "Hmmm? Who coulda helped him? You? Freeman the mad butcher?"

I took a deep, warehouse-cold breath. "Joseph, listen to me. I am profoundly sorry for what we did to you." And I was. The tears were streaming hard, and they were genuine. "I will regret it for all my days. I had no idea! No idea. I was just a kid too, you know. I'm just a little older than you are. Just a few years. I was a kid too. Do you understand that? If there was ever anything I could do to help you, anything I could do to make this right, I would do it. Believe me. Believe that I would."

"Oh...hmmmmm...you can help me all right." Something that almost looked like a 'smile' crept slightly across his face. Then, soon as it came, it was gone, and he was blank again.

"It is 1968, my frien'," he said. "Rev...revolution isss in the air. Hmmm?"

"Huh? What are you talking about?"

"Talking bout a re-volution."

"What...what revolution?"

"Can you sense it? Can you feel it? Hmmm?"

"What revolution, Joseph?"

"So much. So much work to be done."

"What work? What is this shit?"

"Tell me...how is it you've been able to raid the goody closet...to git it in the vein...all these years...and never git caught? Hmmmm? 'Cause you're sly an' crafty?"

"Heh. Sure. Not hardly."

"Iss b'cause they don' notice you. Hmmm. You don' matter to them. Did they ev'r even bother…to learn your name?"

That cut deeper than I wanted to admit.

"What is it you want, Joseph?"

"Can't you sense it? Huhhhh…"

"Fucking madness…"

"I don' dis-agree."

"Tell me! What do you want, Joseph?!"

"What I want? Hmmmmmmm. To burn it all down. Every stone inch."

"Burn what?"

"Set our people free. Hmmmm."

"What the bloody fuck are you talking about?!"

"I am talk'ng bout total de-struction. Burn out the sickness and the rot. Justice. Res…titution. Life is juss a hollow joke, right?"

I nodded slightly, in spite of myself.

"Yeah…Yeah it sure is…"

"Hollow joke…huhhhhhh…"

"It is nothing but one big, pointless mistake," I said. "Yeah. That's it all right."

"Yes…Yes. Unlesss you take control…and make it some…thing else."

"Come again?"

He began to pace about, loping and shifting awkwardly. Though his voice remained a steady machine buzz, his body became progressively more animated with every word.

"You can build what-ever world you choose," he said. "We each have 'at power. Change the world. But…you have to de-stroy the old, rotten world first. And thass juss what we'll do hmmmmm."

"Destroy what? What do you mean *we*?"

"Ev'rything. All the in-stit-utions. Ev'ry lass gah'damn one. Burn the asylums to the ground. Set loose all of our people uponnn the world."

"That's…that's just…"

He put his shaking face right into mine and spat it out in a single, deliberately enunciated breath—

"The schizophrenics, the psychotics, the cannibals and sodomites, the addicts and compulsive self-cutters and nymphomaniacs and people who eat shampoo and masturbate in public…all set free and unleashed upon that 'polite' society out there." He nodded his head frantically. "Hmmmm…They…We…will destroy the hos-pitals…all the hospitals…the churches…the schools…Society will collapse…Ruin. Nothing but ruin. An' there in the rubble, the world will have to face its forgotten childr'n. Its mangled…mutilated…childr'n…"

"Oh god…"

"Every doctor…from pe-dia-tricians to neuro-surgeons…will be strapped down. We will drainnnnnn the power-grid for all the electro-shock machines runn'ng day an' night…curing them all…of their sickness. Hmmmmm…*The cuckoo birds…are coming home.*"

My mind swam. Lost in a sea of gibberish and gobbledygook.

"Now is the time of the assassins…" I whispered.

"Hmmmmmm…" He nodded. "I've read R-Rimbaud too, huuuuh."

Drain the power grid…strap them down…cure the sickness…revolution…

And then at once, it struck me as terribly, ridiculously funny. And I could not help but laugh.

"A lobotomite revolution, huh," I wheezed out an exhausted chuckle. "Heh heh. Wow. Oh Christ. Heh heh heh…OK. Yeah. OK. No offense, Joey…but I just don't see a lobotomite leading an uprising. Sorry. I just don't see it."

"Hmmm…neither do I," he replied, that same faint grin creeping across his lips for a fleeting moment. "Thass where you come innn, Moses."

"My name's not Moses, it's—"

"Your name is Moses now. You are going to huuuuuhhhh…lead

our pe'ple to freedom."

"*Our people?*"

"Hmmmm…"

"*Our people* are not OUR people, pal?"

"Hmmm…huh. You're not a head case, Moses?" he said, jittering excitedly. "You're so trapped in the hospit'l system you might juss as well be a patient. You're as in-stitu-tion-al-ized as anyone I've ev'r met. You think you're not a lobotomite too, Moses? I'd say you are. But you're the only one of us…who cannn ev'r git bett'r. Be healed. An' rise again. Like Jesus. An' you have all the keysss, Moses. All the keys to…all the doors." He reached down and tapped my key ring as it hung from my belt loop. It jingled and clinked, loaded to capacity. "You ARE the key, Moses. To the promised land. You are the key. And you know all the locks…"

"You're…fucking…crazy."

"Yeah. There iss that. Hmmmm. I'm also c'rrect. And you know that, Moses. You know I'm *correct*."

"Nuts."

"Yeah. An' so are you. Hmmm."

"As sure as your name is Doc Hollow…"

"Iss good to have a secret i-dentity, Moses. And some spe'shul gift to offer."

"And I have all the keys…"

"Hmmmm…" he nodded his shaking head. "An' apropos of nothing…I don' have keysss…but I do have *Thorazine*."

With that, I perked straight up.

"What did you say?" *Oh sweet baby Jesus…* "Y-y-you…you're lying," I said, trying not to be betrayed by the hungry quiver in my voice. I failed.

"Am I? Hmmmmm?"

"Come on, don't fuck with me here." He stood nearly still. Just stared through me, shaking. "Come on, man, I'm dying here." Nothing. "I'm fucking dying, Joseph!" Silence, but for a low hum in his throat. "COME ON!!!"

"Don' go anywhere," he said. And with that, he turned on his heel and walked away again.

"No, Joseph, wait! Don't leave me here!"

"You need some time to pond'r...hmmmmm..."

And like a shadow, he disappeared into the darkness.

"Nooooooooooo!!! Come back...come back..."

Alone again. I tried to remember another song to sing. Nothing came.

I tried to draw up some old, fond, faded memory. There were none left at all. There were few to begin with anyhow.

I tried to transport myself to a different time, or place, or body. There was nowhere else to go.

There was nothing on my mind.

I was blank.

And numb.

Hollow.

And only one relentless thought burned like a small candle in my mind—

Revenge.

Retribution.

Revolution...

Hours passed. Or was it days...

There in the vacant nothing of the warehouse I made my peace with the silence. I no longer needed to pull myself away from my reality in the moment. I didn't need the music in my mind. I didn't need escape. I didn't *need* at all.

I found myself. As vacant as the space. As vacant as *this* space. And I embraced the absolute silence.

Until it was shattered.

Somewhere in the distance, I heard an explosion.

And then another.

I heard sirens.

And the *pop pop pop* of discharging firearms.

And I wondered, *Holy shit. Has the boy gone off and lost his patience? Has the lunatic revolution already begun?*

Hours passed. Or was it days...
The violence in the distance was intermittent. But steady. I wondered what it was. It sounded apocalyptic. But far away. I wondered if it would spread closer. I hoped that it would.

Hours passed. Or was it days...
Silence took control again, but for occasional aftershocks of explosions and piercing sirens. When the silence took control, I embraced it absolutely. And I gave direct thought to all of what he had said.
It was then, as I considered him, Joseph Brinkley, *Doc Hollow*...this damaged creature...this destroyed young man...ruined in no small part because of me...it was then, with him out of my direct line of vision, that I think I truly saw him for the first time. A dangerous psychotic? Sure. A raging demon hell-bent on full-scale annihilation? Without a doubt. But also a man with a plan...and I realized at that moment...just how right he was.

Life *is* a mistake, after all. A stupid, random, pointless mistake. A bad cosmic joke. Anything that rips it to pieces could very well be a damn good thing. There was something to be said for complete devastation after all.
And besides, it wasn't the people locked up in the wards who were truly insane. It wasn't them. It was the people locking them up.
It was *everyone else.*
It wasn't the schizophrenics dropping bombs on impoverished rice farmers halfway across the world.
It wasn't the delusional screwballs and shit-throwing nut jobs

siccing attack dogs on little Negro kids down South. Elected officials did that. Perfectly "sane," perfectly "rational." Experts. Leaders. "Very serious people."

Hell, if anyone deserved to be in a padded cell, it was General Westmoreland—

"An' don' f'rget Walter Freeman," I heard Doc Hollow say, invisible, from somewhere deep in the oily darkness. *Goddamn it…I must be thinking out loud again…*

"Joseph!" I called into the black. "Joseph, are you there?"

I thought perhaps, for a moment, that I had truly fallen into the abyss. That I had starting hallucinating his voice. I wondered what time of day it was. But then, I decided that I didn't care anymore. I had lost all concern for that sort of thing.

"OK, Joseph," I said, my eyes burning, sore from exhaustion and salt tears. Now dried out from the cold. And dry from my new peace of mind.

He did not seem to be present, but I said it again anyway—

"OK…" I said.

"OK?"

I heard him, somewhere not too far out of sight.

"OK," I repeated. "Whatever…Whatever you say. Whatever you want, Doc Hollow."

"How's 'at, Moses? Hmmm?"

"I'll do it…whatever you want. Although from the sound of it, you don't need my help burning it all down out there."

"Thass nothing to do with us, Moses," he said, shuffling barely into view, still off in the dim ambient light of the space. "Some scabby fool murder'd a preacher-man in Memmmmphis, Tennessee. Folks have had it. DC's burnnning…hmmmmmm…Columbia Heights…U Street Corridor…Ward 8 is an ocean of flame. Huhhhh."

"Jesus Christ."

"Not the spark I quite had in mind…huhhhh…but I'll take the chaos howev'r it comesss. OK start. Isss an OK start."

"The preacher's dead?"

"You know of 'im?"

"Maybe. From television." I felt as if I should be surprised. "Holy hell…" Or saddened. "It's a shame." But, of course, I wasn't. "He was a good man?" I'll bet he was. And I should have felt a sense of loss. But I couldn't. I didn't feel that sort of thing anymore.

"Likely," he said. "But what doesss it matt'r anyway hmmmm."

"It doesn't matter."

"Huhhhhh…"

"None of it matters."

"Juss more proof of the sickness out there. Hmmm? Iss all comin' downnnn, Moses. Piece by piece. Brick by brick."

"So…" I said, "let's finish the job."

"Once and for allll…"

"I'll help you. I promise. I…I owe it to you."

I owed it to him. I did. I owed it to him.

"Hmmm," he said, sliding fully into view. "Iss not for me, Moses. You owe it…to your pe'ple."

"To *our* people," I said. "To OUR people."

"Hmmm…" He nodded. "For our puhhhh…for our people, you'll do it. You'll make it happ'n…"

"I'll do what I can."

"You'll do what muss be done."

"I'll take a stab at it."

"Yes. Ex-actly hmmmmm…Stab at it…"

"*Moses*, huh?" I asked.

"It fits you."

"*Fuck the Pharaoh*," I said. "Fuck him straight through the eye."

"I like 'at. I like it a lot."

"But you're the brains here," I said.

"Thass…ironic…"

"When the time is right," I said, "I'll introduce you to the world. They need to know. They need to know *you*. They need to know who you are. They need to recognize."

"*Ladies an' gennl'man…huhhhhh…*"
"Just one thing, Joseph."
"Hmmmm?"
"I sure do gotta piss, and no foolin'."
With that, he ambled behind me, jerking and twitching with an insectile gait.
That's all it took?!
He pulled out a pocketknife from his rain jacket, and tried to saw through the ropes on my wrists. Not much luck. Too dull. He removed my buck knife from its holster and gave that a go. It sliced right through.
I stood up, shaky on my legs just yet. Dizzy, and lightheaded. But oddly light in spirit as well, what little of it I had left. Buoyed by the thought of destroying the world. In order to save it. It made sense. It felt right. I nodded to him, and began walking toward what looked like a doorway.
"You know the score, Moses?" he said, "Huhhhh? You runnn, an' so do I. From what you've seen nnnnow, you really want that chasing you the ress of your life?"
"I'm not running, Doc," I said. "I'm not running. I'm with you."
I walked out into a stone alley and into the cool DC air. It was black as pitch outside, but for a small smattering of stars. I couldn't read the darkness, though. I had no sense of if twilight had just faded, or if dawn was just around the corner.
I saw smoke and flame rising in the distance, likely from Washington Highlands. I peeled off my vomit-encrusted shirt and tossed it into the gravel. It was a chilly April in DC, but no matter.
I took care of business against the jagged cinderblock of an opposing wall, and my eyes adjusted further to the darkness. Nothing in any direction but an industrial black hole of warehouses and rusted machinery. I felt as though my inner compass was finally resetting. *That must surely be the Highlands over there on fire*, I thought. But I couldn't be sure. I had been so focused on Irina on the way there, that I had not noticed where exactly we were.

Served me right, after all. I let myself get sloppy. Pretend for one second like the world isn't out to get you, and that's exactly when it lays you out with a sucker punch.

I did briefly entertain the notion of making a break for it. But to where could I run? Who would listen? Who would believe me? And how long before *The Transorbitals* came for me again? How long could I fight them off? Forever? That strength was not mine.

I imagined all the kids I had seen up on Pennsylvania Avenue just a few days prior, camped out on the sidewalk. Begging Uncle Sam not to send them off to kill and die for no good fucking reason. *Best of luck there, kids.* Did I 'get' their groove? Where did I belong? And with whom? *Bet they've all run off by now…*

I thought about the folks setting fire to their world all around me, just out of sight. And I thought about the swells and politicos and fat cats all hiding, cowering in their high towers, likely calling up the Guards to "settle this problem." To gun the crazies down. And I thought, *So many cages. So many cages.*

We're all locked up. Every single one of us, institutionalized. I used to hate when people referred to the patients in psychiatric hospitals as "inmates." But that's exactly what they are. *And so are we all.*

Where do I belong? Who do I belong with?
THE SICK.
That is what I am. That is who I am.
It's all just one big asylum. And it needs to be burned to the ground.

As I walked back inside the warehouse, up the metal staircase and back into the space, I saw Doc Hollow waiting. Down at the far end. Waiting for me. He was not alone. Sitting upright in the chair I had just previously vacated, just as proper as you please, was a figure very, very familiar to me.

"Walter?"

"Oh, hello, lad," he said, pleasantly enough. "My my, twice in a week? Have we traveled back in time you and I?"

He appeared completely unfazed by the situation. Calm, like he was always calm, as if we were simply having a Sunday get-together, his hands folded neatly in his lap. From his demeanor one might be forgiven for assuming that he was there of his own volition.

"What the hell's going on here?" I asked as I walked toward them as quickly as I my wobbly legs were able. It wasn't until I was but a few feet away that I saw his wrists were bound with raw twine.

Freeman turned to Doc Hollow with a curt but friendly nod. "And hello to you, Joseph. The discourteous treatment from your friends notwithstanding, it is good to see you. How are we feeling?"

"Spare me your bedside mann'r, Freeman," said Doc Hollow, swaying back and forth with a nervous urgency.

"Still with the anger issues, alas," Freeman sighed, "But we have made some progress, don't you think?"

"You'll know I've made progressss…when your world is noth'ng but smold'ring wreckage…an' elec-tricity iss blasting through your colleagues."

"Just give it time," Freeman said to him, a bland smile spread across his lips. "Perhaps just a day or so in fact." He cleared his throat. "I spoke with your father the other day, Joseph," he said. "He fears he's getting too old to look after you. Do you understand what that means, Joseph? Should we perhaps start looking into a facility for you? They run a tight ship over at St. Agnes. I've seen to that."

Doc Hollow turned to me with a flapping, accusatory finger toward Walter.

"Do you see thisss, Moses? Do you hear…this meg-alomaniac? Is this your sup'rhero? Hmmm?"

"I, of course, feel as I always have," Walter continued casually, "that with a bit more effort on your part, Joseph, you could function just fine in a low-stress environment. Shelving books at a library perhaps. Or taking tickets at the picture show. Does any of that sound appealing to you, Joseph?"

"He muss be stopped, Moses," Hollow hissed to me, "Thisss lunatic muss be stopped." I didn't respond. I felt detached from the proceedings, and very near collapse. I wondered if there was any more water left in the thermos. Or if Doc Hollow really had Thorazine on his person.

"Did he ev'r tell you, Moses," said Doc Hollow, "about Annabel Johnson?"

"Ah yes," Walter said. "Poor little Annabel. That was a sad loss." That is what he said. He did not seem particularly sad. "Truly unfortunate to be sure."

"You murder'd an eight-year-old girl, Freeman." Hollow's monotone murmur began to evolve into a rattling growl. "You stabbed her…in th' brain…with a metal spike. An' she died."

Freeman nodded in resignation. "The science is indeed imprecise after all."

Hollow's face remained blank, but his body shook. An angry rope of spit began to descend from his bottom lip.

"Thiss monst'r muss be neu-tralized, Moses. Step one to th' revolution. Hmmmmmmm. You muss neutral-ize him. It iss your job, Moses."

I knew I should respond, but at the moment, I was just a bit short on words.

"Yeah?" I said faintly. "Step one?"

"You muss do it."

"He's got cancer, Joseph," I said, looking to Freeman to see if he would appear surprised that I knew. He did not. "Life will neutralize him in time. We can be sure of that."

"This is true," Freeman offered. "No outside help is really necessary."

"You know hisss crimes, Moses," Hollow pressed further. "You know…huhhhhhhh…you know he muss be punish'd."

We stood in silence for a while. The ball was in my court. No getting around that fact. I'd have to be the one.

"Yes," I said finally. "Yes. He must be punished."

"He'ss a murder'r. Hmmm. That world out there…doesn' punish doctors for their crimes, Mosesss. So we muss…make them pay."

TRANSORBITAL

"Make them pay…"
"The f'gotten and the mu-tilated will fin'lly have justice."
"Justice…"
"And the beast…muss be destroyed."
"Must be destroyed…The beast…must be destroyed…"

Hollow walked over to me, his jagged, beat-less steps deliberate and final. He handed me the pick and the mallet. I took them, and I walked over slowly toward Walter, still a bit uneasy on my legs as well. Doc Hollow did likewise, and stood behind Doc Freeman. He removed Freeman's spectacles from his face and dropped them unceremoniously to on the floor.

"Careful now," Walter said.

Joseph pried both of Walter's eyelids open with his fingers and thumbs. It was a grotesque sight no doubt, and one that nearly made me laugh.

"Do it, Moses," Doc Hollow said. "You know this iss right. It iss what muss be done. Hmmmmm. First step to the revolution. Walter Freeman muss be done away with. Once an' for all. Come on, Moses. *Hollow him out.*"

I looked at the mallet and orbitoclast in my hands. *Freeman original.*

"That is a quality instrument," Walter said, his eyes comically wide and round against his will.

"You really are a monster, Doc," I said, but I don't really know to whom. "You really are a goddamn monster."

"He needs hisss med'cine," said Hollow through his teeth, "Give it to 'im. You don' even…have to kill him. You actu'lly know how to do it right, hmmmm? Death iss too good for him, Moses."

I looked down on Walter sitting there, eyes pried open by black-gloved fingers. I looked to the spike, and I looked back again. I thought about all of what he had done. What WE had done. And for a brief moment I entertained the notion of turning the orbitoclast on myself. I wondered if it would be possible to self-administer a transorbital lobotomy. It would be the first of its kind, no doubt about that. Groundbreaking. Revolutionary.

But I leaned over Walter instead, pointing the tip right above his right eye, into the dark blood-pink of the socket.

"Go ahead, lad," he said. "You know what to do."

I slowly eased the pick toward Freeman's eye socket, thinking to myself, *In all the years I've been a part of the procedure, I've never actually operated the spike myself...*

Well, you have to start sometime.

"You can do it, lad," Freeman said, "it's just an ice pick."

With all the strength I had left, I jabbed the pick forward, straight past Freeman's head, and stabbed Doc Hollow dead in the stomach.

Hollow released Freeman with a gasp, but otherwise remained expressionless. With a quick pivot, I ran behind him, swung him around and skewered him over and over again in the kidneys. Over and over and over. And over again. Fifteen times? Twenty? I lost count. I just kept stabbing, mindlessly, too afraid to stop.

"My word," I heard Dr. Freeman say.

I had to do it. He had threatened Doctor Freeman, after all...

"What an awful waste," Dr. Freeman said, clucking his tongue.

...And love him or hate him, Doctor Freeman was my captain. My alpha. My superhero. Right or wrong...

"Such a shame."

So I just kept on stabbing...

"Such a terrible shame."

Hollow stumbled toward the ground, spilling blood across the warehouse floor. I realized that I had not been breathing, and opened my mouth to suck in new air. In the process I fell to the floor vomiting, retching out what little I had left in my gut. We were drained. We were both drained. All over the floor.

I felt Hollow grab the collar of my cold, sweat-soaked undershirt and pull me to the floor. He grabbed a hold of my head, but I had not the strength left to fight him off.

"This doesn'...end here," he wheezed into my ear, coughing blood against my cheek. "It begins now. With you. You said it y'rself...the rev-olution...will nev'r be lead...by a lobotomite.

You know the truth an'…you have the power. And you're healed now. All healed now. You have the keysss…to the asylum. All of the asylums." His voice began to clip as he faded away. "Fuck the Pharaoh, Moses. Fuck him…with ann ice pick to th' brain. Hmmm…Iss in your hand, Moses. Set…our…people free…"

He was gone. And, but for the fact that he was no longer shaking, he didn't look much different stone dead.

I crawled upright onto my knees, pulled Joseph's knife from his pocket and tried to cut Doc Freeman loose. No good. I pulled out my buck knife and that made short work of it. Another repeat of another pointless ritual.

Freeman stood, dusting himself off.

"Blasted," he said as he bent down to pick up his glasses from the floor, now not just scratched to hell, but cracked straight through both lenses.

I pulled myself up from the floor and took his seat. I let my head hang back. I felt paralyzed again, trapped in one of my static nightmares. But I could breathe. I could breathe fully. At least I could breathe.

"Well, that was certainly less than pleasant," Doc Freeman said, rubbing his rope-burned wrists. "All right then, lad?"

I nodded as best I could.

"So…I'll just be phoning the police then," he said. "I'm sure that their hands are a bit tied with all of this riot business, but they'll get to it in time. And I'll be sure to tell them that you handled the situation with aplomb."

"Yeah…" I said. "Aplomb…"

"Sad about Joseph Brinkley," he said with a *tsk tsk tsk*. "I really had hopes for that one."

I nodded again.

"Hopes…"

"Well, it was good to see you, lad," he said, moseying on toward the doorway at the far north end of the warehouse. "Don't be a stranger now. Perhaps we can meet for dinner sometime soon. Yes?"

"Sure. Sure thing, Doc."

"Splendid. Just phone my office, all right?"

"Sure thing, Doc."

"So…until then, fair thee well. Oh, and do take care of yourself, yes? Keep your powder dry and your nose clean. Don't get stuck in a fix."

And with that, he took his leave.

Without fully realizing what I was doing, I got back down onto the floor, patting around on Joseph Brinkley's raincoat. I felt a hard lump in his left side pocket that rattled when I tapped it. I reached in and pulled out a small bottle of chlorpromazine hydrochloride capsules.

You think you're not a lobotomite too? You think you're not a head case?

I stuffed the bottle into my pocket, along with Joseph's knife. No such thing as too many knives after all.

I found myself slowly cleaning the bloody leucotome on my undershirt. I pocketed that as well, along with the mallet.

I unhooked the key ring from my belt. Loaded to capacity with keys. *So many cupboards and closets…so many doors…so many cages…*I studied them intently for a moment, very methodically eyeing one, then the next, as if I'd never really looked at them before. Never really considered their power. Perhaps I hadn't. Indeed I had not. *Couldn't speak too much beyond my own routine these days, you understand*, but I have been meaning to pick up on what's going down out there. It seemed pretty heavy. *So many cages…*And now…now I understood. *Now I understand.* Finally. *So many asylum doors.* And I knew what I had to do. *I'm so far behind now. There's so much. So much.* So much work to be done.

Well…off to work.

ACKNOWLEDGMENTS

Thank you to Mom and Dad and the ever-growing horde that is our family. To Paul Anderson, Philip Rogers, Stephanie & Eric Beebe and the entire Post Mortem Press gang. To Eric Campbell, Lance Wright and all of the good folks at Down & Out Books—it's been great working with you on this project. To The Whiskey Shambles krewe, the Carian clan, The Starshaker posse, the Performance Gallery tribe, and all the other misfits and weirdoes who like to make a scene and a spectacle with us in public. To Mike Magnuson, Alison Dasho. Tasha Alexander, JD Rhoades, Laure Manceau, Judith Vernant, Ben LeRoy, Gary Heidt, Yishai Seidman, Marcus Sakey, John Connolly, Frank Bill, Ben Whitmer, Tyler McMahon, Greg Petersen, Andrew Nienaber, Anne Peralta, Che'Rae Adams, Alisa Tangredi, Michelle Lema, Doug Oliphant, Shawn MacAulay, Matt Ryan, William Salyers, John Schumacher, Mary Jo McClain, Bryon Quertermous, Steve Weddle, Reed Farrel Coleman, and everyone at the Los Angeles Writers Center. And to Peter Streicher (Rest In Peace). My deepest apologies to anyone I forgot to mention. First round is on me.

Nathan Singer is a novelist, playwright, composer, and experimental performing artist. He is also the lead vo-calist and guitarist for award-winning "ultra-blues" band The Whiskey Shambles. His published novels are the controversial and critically-acclaimed *A Prayer for Dawn, Chasing the Wolf, In the Light of You, The Song in the Squall,* and *Transorbital.* He currently lives in Cincinnati, Ohio where he is working on a multi-tude of new projects.

Down & Out Books

On the following pages are a few
more great titles from the
Down & Out Books publishing family.

For a complete list of books and to
sign up for our newsletter,
go to DownAndOutBooks.com.

Occam's Razor
Joe Clifford

Down & Out Books
June 2020
978-1-64396-106-4

Former NFL prospect Oz Reyes is summoned to Miami by his boss, Delma Dupree, who asks him to investigate what she calls "the wrongful imprisonment" of her stepson.

With the help of an ex-girlfriend her ex-convict brother, Oz uncovers a South Florida rarely seen, one crawling with shifty detectives, rogue assassins, and hard-drinking, sexual deviants—where no one and nothing is what it seems.

Together They Were Crimson
Ryan Sayles

Down & Out Books
July 2020
978-1-64396-037-1

An Angel of Mercy serial killer targets the elderly, but when a visitor catches her in the act, the Angel is forced to murder her.

Norm Braden, the victim's widower, is grieving for his lost wife and struggling to hold his family together. The killer visits Norm, claims she hasn't been feeling right since, Norm says, "It's guilt. "You feel guilty for what you did."

Norm seeks revenge. The Angel seeks some form of completion she sees in him. And their cat-and-mouse game begins.

The Akerman Motel/Apartments per week
Part Four of the Trevor English Series
Pablo D'Stair

All Due Respect, an imprint of
Down & Out Books
July 2020
978-1-64396-109-5

Laying low in a cold water flat, petty crook Trevor English inadvertently discovers the truth behind a violent crime. Taking no action against the perpetrator, he is nevertheless accused of holding the information over their head.

And despite his claims of non-involvement, Trevor soon finds he must either play fall-guy to the crime or else pay out someone else's blackmail to keep his own past from being raked up.

White Trash and Dirty Dingoes
Jason Parent

Shotgun Honey, an imprint of
Down & Out Books
July 2020
978-1-64396-101-9

Gordon thought he'd found the girl of his dreams. But women like Sarah are tough to hang on to.

When she causes the disappearance of a mob boss's priceless Chihuahua, she disappears herself, and the odds Gordon will see his lover again shrivel like nuts in a polar plunge.

With both money and love lost, he's going to have to kill some SOBs to get them back.

Made in the USA
Columbia, SC
25 September 2024